D1113859

SANTUKKAH!

MIDDLE SCHOOL MAYHEM 2

C.T. WALSH

FARCICAL PRESS

COVER CREDITS

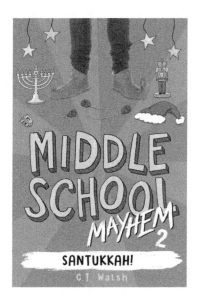

Publisher's Cataloging-in-Publication Data

provided by Five Rainbows Cataloging Services

Names: Walsh, C.T., author.

Title: Santukkah! / C.T. Walsh.

Description: Bohemia, NY : Farcical Press, 2019. | Series: Middle school mayhem, bk 2. | Summary: Jealous of his brother's sports success, Austin tries out for the school musical but has to compete with the new boy in town. | Audience: Grades 5 & up. | Also available in ebook and audiobook formats.

Identifiers: ISBN 978-1-950826-00-1 (paperback)

Subjects: LCSH: Bildungsromans. | CYAC: Middle school students--Fiction. | Middle schools--Fiction. | Jealousy--Fiction. | Musicals--Fiction. | Bullying--Fiction. | Humorous stories. | BISAC: JUVENILE FICTION / Social Themes / Adolescence & Coming of Age. | JUVENILE FICTION / School & Education. | JUVENILE FICTION / Humorous Stories. | JUVENILE FICTION / Boys & Men.

Classification: LCC PZ7.1.W35 San 2019 (print) | LCC PZ7.1.W35 (ebook) | DDC [Fic]--dc23.

For my Family

Thank you for all of your support

1

Mayhem [*mey*-hem] noun: A state of rowdy disorder. Better known as middle school. Well, at least mine: Cherry Avenue. I know it sounds all sweet and cuddly, like you just want to pinch its cheeks and make a bunch of strange baby sounds like a weirdo, but you've got to believe me. It's all a bunch of false marketing designed to trick parents into believing that our middle school is a nurturing sanctuary of educational excellence, when, in fact, it's a swamp of tween drama, body odor, and rancid beef. I should probably tell you the whole story, just to make sure you're convinced.

Austin Davenport here and this is my story, with a few fart jokes sprinkled in (and sometimes blasted). Now, you're certainly entitled to your own opinion, but we're gonna get along a lot better if you just accept that I'm the hero of this story. There's really no other way to interpret it, as far as I'm concerned, but some people have a screw loose or might be mesmerized by the optical illusion created by the depth of my brother Derek's butt chin.

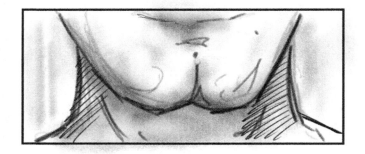

Others may be easily hoodwinked by Randy Warblemacher's Ken-doll good looks or even blinded by Principal Buthaire's oversized mustache. He says his name all snooty and French, like "Booo-tare," but you can probably imagine that us middle schoolers prefer to call him, "Butt Hair," or more formally, "Principal Butt Hair." I mean, not to his face, because that would just be plain rude.

It was November 2nd, the first day back at school after the Halloween dance. If you haven't heard that story, let me just tell you, it was awesome. For me, anyway. But the aftermath? Not so much. Let's just say that when you create a storm, don't be surprised when it rains. Or floods, which was more apt to the situation I was in. I probably should've thought about that before I battled our prison warden/principal, but sometimes a hero doesn't get to choose his time to rise. Events just unfold and the hero is born. To be honest, I was as surprised as everyone else. I'm not your typical hero. I don't have the family butt chin. Brains, snark, and embarrassing myself in front of girls are my superpowers.

Anyway, Principal Buthaire was on the warpath. My friends and I had thwarted his every move to crush our sweet souls. He was determined to find the perpetrators that stopped his evil plot to flood the Halloween dance and turned it into a foam party and I was prime suspect number one. I'm not a bad kid, mind you. But sometimes you have to fight fire with foam. And a Sharpie. The perpetrators also allegedly drew a mustache on a picture of his wife after breaking into his office, The Butt Crack, as it is affectionately known. It was my best artistic work. Allegedly.

Principal Buthaire stood before our entire Phys Ed class, pacing the immaculately-waxed floor as we sat in the bleachers. Mr. Muscalini stood next to him, teary eyed and squeezing a stress ball, muttering, "No pain, no gain," over and over.

Class was on hold until Principal Buthaire interrogated each and every one of us and that just didn't work for Mr. Muscalini. I didn't mind gym being shut down, but I was a little nervous about getting in trouble. Principal Buthaire was likely going to win the Nobel Prize at the end of the year for giving out detentions. Two months into the year, I was his go-to guy, and he was looking for me again.

Ben Gordon, my best friend, leaned over to me and whispered, "Don't let him break you. Admit nothing." He shrugged. "At least that's what they say in the movies."

I nodded, as Principal Buthaire eyed me with disgust.

"Good morning," he said to our class as if it were the worst morning he'd ever experienced. "As you may know, hooligans flooded and nearly destroyed this gym on Friday night at the Halloween dance, not to mention broke into the main office and Mr. Zorch's storage facility. Without the excellent work of Mr. Zorch, this gym could've been damaged beyond repair."

Mr. Muscalini let out a tiny whimper. A few kids snickered, which was quickly met by Principal Buthaire's laser eyes.

"A pity," I whispered to Ben. I'm not too keen on things of an athletic nature.

Principal Buthaire locked his eyes on mine and continued, "The perpetrators will be caught and expelled!"

Eyes widened throughout the bleachers. My heart thumped even though I knew what he didn't. I could expose his plot to take down the dance, possibly costing him his job. But I wasn't willing to risk getting kicked out of school, as much as I hated it, because I knew the alternative. My father threatens my brother, Derek, with military school at least once a week. I feared that would be my fate. And that was a fate I would not survive.

"Admit your participation now and you will only be suspended for a month. If I have to find out on my own, and I *will* find out, I will expel you." There were a solid forty kids in the bleachers, but as far as Principal Buthaire was concerned, I was the only one. He continued, "We already have a lot of pieces that are coming together."

I looked around at my classmates. Even kids who had nothing to do with the whole thing were scared.

"If you have any information that helps my investigation, you will be given get-out-of-detention free passes."

Wow. He was serious and possibly desperate. With all of

the detentions that Principal Buthaire gives out, a free pass was worth more than gold, at least to middle school kids who have no use for gold.

"Let's start with you, Mr. Gerard."

Jimmy Gerard, normally a tough athlete, and one that had nothing to do with any of this debacle, looked like he was on his way to his own funeral. His shoulders slumped as he walked toward a table and two folding chairs set off to the side of the gym. Principal Buthaire joined him at the table and began the interrogation.

One by one, Principal Buthaire pulled students aside and questioned them about their whereabouts on the night of the dance and their knowledge of foam machines. Given the collection of meat heads in our class, the list of suspects was going to get narrowed down really quick. I sat in the bleachers, biting my nails and waiting for my turn.

"Hey, Gordo. You're up next," Mr. Muscalini said, pointing to Principal Buthaire and then caught sight of his own bicep. He smiled and admired it like a father seeing his baby for the first time. I was surprised he didn't start kissing it. It wouldn't have been the first time.

Ben stood up and whispered shakily, "Stay strong." I hoped he would take his own advice.

I was the last one left. And that was by design. I'm sure Principal Buthaire wanted me to sweat, not to mention to have as much information about what might have happened so that he could expel me by lunch. Chicken Surprise was on the menu, so I wasn't sure what to hope for.

"Davenport," Mr. Muscalini nodded to me. "You're up next." He frowned. "You know Derek Davenport?"

"Yes. He's my brother." I'd told him that at least twenty times before. Apparently, it just didn't compute. And I didn't really blame him. We were so different.

"You sure?"

"Yep, pretty sure. I've been living with him for almost eleven years." My birthday was a month away. I would turn eleven in December while Derek would turn twelve in January.

I was trying to read Ben's facial expressions, but Mr. Muscalini kept interrupting me. "Are you adopted?"

I shook my head with a huff. "No, Mr. Muscalini. I just stink at sports and I don't have a butt on my chin."

He was a little taken aback. He studied my nondescript chin and nodded. I caught Ben moving out of the corner of my eye. He stood up and eyed me. If he was trying to tell me something, he wasn't doing a very good job.

"Good luck, Davenport," Mr. Muscalini said, still scratching his head.

I walked over and slumped into the chair across from my nemesis. Principal Buthaire narrowed his eyes, as he looked me up and down. "I know it was you," he said, matter-of-factly.

I shook my head. "I had nothing to do with it," I lied. "You might want to talk to my brother, though." I knew he wouldn't because he already had. They were in on the whole thing together. I had heard them plot it while I was hiding under his desk in his office, The Butt Crack. It's a long story. I looked up at Principal Buthaire. "I'm sure this all goes back to him. Can I have my free pass now?"

Principal Buthaire laughed, but more at me than with me, because I wasn't laughing at all. "I spoke to Mr. Gifford. He said there are only a handful of students capable of building a foam machine of that magnitude. And two of them were you and Mr. Gordon."

I shrugged casually, but my pulse was pounding. "Yeah, I'm smart, but that doesn't mean I did any of it. Plus, dumb kids have access to YouTube. And who says it wasn't kids from Bear Creek? They're always messing with us around homecoming time."

He studied me without speaking. I didn't want to show weakness or any hint of guilt. I stared right back at him. "I don't like you, Mr. Davenport."

I didn't know how to respond to that, but I felt like it meant I was winning. I decided to needle him a little. I played dumb. "Sir, shouldn't the video cameras have caught the perpetrator on tape?"

Principal Buthaire looked like he might be sick. "Unfortunately, the system was down due to a software error."

"Too bad," I said, knowing full well that I was the one who erased the software after breaking into his office.

"We are investigating the source of that error as we speak," he said, hopeful.

I didn't like the sound of that, but it appeared as if he had little or no evidence about either incident, so I was likely in the clear. And then thankfully, the bell rang. Class was over. I stood up and looked at Principal Buthaire expectantly. He didn't say anything.

"Sir, I need to get to my next class."

"We're finished when I say we're finished." He stared at me for a moment. "I'm watching you, Mr. Davenport."

Not without your cameras, I thought.

"Sit down," he said, sternly.

I slid back into my chair. I looked over at the rest of my classmates who were rushing toward the exits.

I stared at Principal Buthaire, waiting for him to say something. Anything. "Sir, I'm going to be late."

He acted like he hadn't heard me say anything. He checked his watch, straightened his tie, and tapped his fingers on the table.

Three minutes later, the bell rang. It was the longest three minutes of my life. "You can go now," he said.

"Can I have a late pass?" I asked.

Principal Buthaire smiled. "Oh, you're late." He traced his mustache with his fingers. "Detention!" he yelled at the top of his lungs.

"You forced me to be here!"

He tore off a detention slip from his pad and handed it to me. I bit my tongue, knowing it wasn't a great time to ask if his vendetta against me was worth single handedly destroying the environment. I grabbed the slip, stuffed it into my pocket, and hustled off in a huff.

Principal Buthaire called after me, "Have a lovely day, Mr. Davenport!" His evil cackle echoed throughout the gym.

THE REST of my day was pretty uneventful. After school, I finished my homework and then played video games. I was looking forward to a quiet and relaxing night with some tasty snacks and more video games, when my mom walked into the den and ruined it with, "Austin, geez. Let's get a move on! Get your jacket and tie on. Tonight's Derek's big night!"

I dropped my controller on the floor, as my will to live shriveled up. I'd totally forgotten about it. Perhaps, blocked it out of my mind was a better way to describe it. My brother was getting the Cherry Avenue Middle School football team Rookie of the Year award.

"Do I really have to go?" I whined.

I had no interest in being there. The only thing Derek was better at than sports was tormenting me. We had come to a recent truce after he had spent the prior decade plundering my spirit, but that doesn't mean I forgave him for any of it.

"Yes. This is a big deal. We're very proud of him. Now, hurry."

I fell to the floor into a heap of anger. Eventually, my mom's nagging forced me to find the strength to stand up and mope to my room. Not only was I lucky enough to get to wear and suit and tie to a rubber chicken dinner, I also got to sit through three hours of athletic awards, one of which was meant for my brother. Yay!

The banquet hall was packed with jocks and their families. It was an awards dinner for the fall middle and high school sporting teams, with a special emphasis on football, our town's baby. Need money for a club, science fair, or food for needy children? Get in line. Need money for football? They open up the bank vault. It's not fair. What's worse, they didn't even offer soda. The only thing they had was protein shakes. Unbelievable.

It was virtually insufferable from the first minute when Mr. Muscalini stepped up to the microphone. He wore a shirt, tie, and gym shorts. He said, "Welcome. For those of you who don't know, I was the county ping pong champion in 1992, proudly wearing our green and gold. And all I got was a paper certificate. There were no interviews, no newspaper articles, no visits to the White House. Not even a plastic trophy. I felt slighted. My dignity evaporated. I slipped into a deep depression. I wondered if my mother still loved me."

Mr. Muscalini appeared to be crying. Over table tennis. I looked at my parents to see if any of Mr. Muscalini's nonsense made any sense to them. It did not appear so.

Mr. Muscalini continued, "So I vowed to never let that happen to anyone else! We will celebrate our successes with gargantuan trophies so that no Gopher child in the green and gold will ever experience what I had to endure. To question a mother's love..." After a few sniffles he continued, "Our first award goes to..."

I passed out from complete and utter boredom. I woke up seven minutes later to cheers for the cross country team, who apparently doesn't even come close to running anywhere near across the country. The whole thing was a lie. I looked over at my parents and asked, "Is this over yet?"

My mother shushed me. Shushed me! I shook my head and stared at the ceiling.

The awards ceremony hit minute one hundred and sixty seven, but who's counting? It turned out that every bored sibling was, at least those that were able to maintain consciousness. I think my sister Leighton's eyes rolled back in her head a few times.

Mr. Muscalini stood atop the stage, his muscles nearly ripping through his dress shirt like the Hulk as he held a ginormous golden trophy. He raised the microphone and said, "Our next award goes to an up-and-coming football star. We call him the King of Quick and Señor Speed. Show your Gopher pride for our middle school football Rookie of the Year, Derek, The Destroyer, Davenport!"

The banquet hall exploded into applause. Some even stood up to cheer. My mom started to tear up. Geez, lady. Get it together. I pretended it was all for me for putting up with my brother for all those years. The crowd's applause and cheers were so loud, it was invigorating and energizing, even though it really wasn't for me, but for my butt-chinned brother. I had never felt that way before. I wanted that same feeling and those cheers for me.

My brother strutted up to the stage, his hair perfectly messy, his tie coolly loose, and his butt chin bared for all the world to see. He was grinning from ear to ear. He ran up the steps, waving to the crowd. He shook hands with Mr. Muscalini and then waved again to the rest of us little people.

Mr. Muscalini clapped him on the back as he held out the shiny trophy. Derek grabbed the oversized trophy, which looked like it was solid gold, and thrust it over his head to more cheers. He grabbed the microphone from Mr. Muscalini and said, "Thank you for this award. It is much deserved. I worked hard for this." Wow. His humility was inspiring. He admired the trophy. I thought he might kiss it. He looked over at our table, "It wouldn't have been possible without the support of my parents, my sister, Leighton, and-" At least after enduring the boring blubber fest, he was going to thank me...or not. He continued, "...all of you for cheering us on every week from the sidelines."

I was disgusted. I stood up and walked out. I don't think anyone from my family even noticed. I needed some fresh air. It turns out, I wasn't the only one. I found myself toe to toe with none other than my nemesis, the unprincipled Principal Buthaire.

"Well, hello, Austin," he said, monotone.

"Hi," I whispered and walked past, hoping I would get away without being given detention for breathing in the hallway.

"Enjoying the festivities?"

I stopped and turned around. I wasn't sure if I actually had to speak to him, but I didn't want to risk it. "Not really."

"It's a pity that you aren't enjoying your last evening of freedom."

My eyes nearly popped out of my head. I looked at him, confused. Was I getting shipped off to juvenile prison? Military school? I stammered, "I...I don't understand, sir."

"Well, let me make it clear for you. I know what you did at the dance and I am going to press charges for destruction of property and criminal mischief."

Ah, farts. "I had nothing to do with any of that. Talk to the golden boy inside. You might want to make an appointment. He's a celebrity now."

I forced a smile and walked away, my heart thumping in my ears. I didn't know what to do, but between Principal Buthaire and Derek The Destroyer, I needed to get out of there. I pushed the doors open to the courtyard and slinked into the shadow. It took every ounce of strength I had to keep from breaking down into tears.

The car ride wasn't any easier. On the way home, Derek was even more insufferable than usual. I sat in the middle seat between him and Leighton, with my parents in the front of the SUV. We thought we were going to have to leave Derek behind because his big head almost didn't fit inside. Fresh off the football victory, he was already focused on his next conquest.

"Man, that was awesome. Standing ovation! The King of Quick...Derek the Destroyer. Mr. Muscalini said I could be the first sixth grader to win a starting hoops spot on the middle school team."

"That's great, honey," my mom said.

"You just have to work on going left with your dribble," my father added.

"I know, Dad," Derek said, annoyed.

"Just give it your best, bud. That's all that matters," Dad said.

Derek leaned forward, his overpriced and oversized trophy jabbing me in the knee.

"Oww, get that thing off me!" I yelled. In hindsight, I may have overreacted. I shoved it back onto his lap.

"Easy, jerk!" Derek yelled. "I'm sorry. It's so big. I don't know what to do with it." He jabbed me in the ribs with a punch. I wanted to retaliate, but it hurt so much and I don't usually win those battles. Or never.

"Boys..." my father said, looking at us in the rear-view mirror.

Derek went right back to his obnoxious self. "Starting hoops *and* football rookie of the year!"

"Big deal, butt nugget," I muttered to myself.

"It is a big deal!" Derek yelled. "And I'm not a butt nugget!"

"That's debatable. The rest of us really don't care that God gave you the ability to run fast. He gave Dad a hairy back. Let's give him an award!"

Leighton chimed in, "Both of you, shut up!"

"Enough!" My dad said and then whispered to my mom, "Is my back really that hairy?"

My mom nodded and then turned to us in the back seat. "Keep your hands and trophies to yourselves and your mouths shut." I didn't mind getting yelled it, because it meant Derek would finally stop talking. That's how I loathed him the least.

When we got home, I went straight for my room, locked the door, and ignored everyone as much as humanly possible until I left for school the next day.

I WALKED into school the next morning, still frustrated. Principal Buthaire greeted students in the hallway with a broad smile. My mood soured even more. He caught my eye and waved. I frowned in confusion. And then I realized why he was so happy. I saw two technicians adjusting security cameras off in the distance in the atrium. His detention-giving capabilities were heading back to full life-ruining capacity.

Principal Buthaire pointed to his eyes, then to me, and mouthed, "I'm watching you."

On the bright side, November started a new marking period, which meant new classes. I added music to my schedule. And my girlfriend, Sophie, and Ben were in my class. I sat in the middle row between them. Most of the class had settled in, but a few students burst through the door as the bell rang, getting stuck in the door jam. They quickly rejiggered themselves through the door and found seats. A tall woman with a yellow gown entered. She smiled and said, "Good morning. Mrs. Funderbunk will begin shortly." She set her pocketbook down on the desk.

Sophie leaned over and whispered, "Who is she?" I shrugged and looked around the room. Everyone seemed a little confused.

The woman fluffed out her long, black hair and straightened her oversized glasses. "Mrs. Funderbunk is ready for you now."

Ben raised his hand. "When will Mrs. Funderbunk be arriving?"

"She and I are one and the same." Mrs. Funderbunk smiled. "Welcome to music! Allow me to introduce myself. I am Madeline Funderbunk!" She said it with such gusto a few kids started to clap like she was famous or something.

"Oh, children. You're too kind. Stop it," Mrs. Funderbunk feigned embarrassment. She took a deep breath and continued, "Actually, a little more would be quite okay with me." A

fter the applause died down, she said, "Les Mis, A Chorus line, Cats, Phantom of the Opera, and... Santukkah!" She gestured with her hands like it was on a Broadway marquee sign.

We were all confused. Anna LaValle asked, "What's that?"

Mrs. Funderbunk eyed her like she was the dumbest kid in school. "It's the next Hamilton, going to take Broadway by storm."

"But what is it?" Anna asked again.

"It's Santukkah!" Mrs. Funderbunk gestured the marquee again. "It's a holiday mashup, written and directed by moí."

"Who's moí?" Ben asked.

Mrs. Funderbunk shook her head. "I forget how uncultured we are these days. It's French. It means me. Sixth graders might not be aware, but we do our own holiday pageant. I wrote this year's extravaganza, called Santukkah! which celebrates the holiday season in all its glory. Let's get right into it. Everyone stand, please."

The class stood up. "We'll start with some warm ups. Repeat after me." She sang, "Sam saw Sally sweating at the swanky shoe shop."

We sang the line as she paced in front of us. "Good," she said and then sang, "Dan donned a dashing, dark diaper with diamonds and doodies in Denmark."

I looked over at Sophie and frowned. She shrugged. It was ridiculous, but we sang it anyway.

Mrs. Funderbunk nodded as she assessed our tune. "Freddy farted in Frankfort, frightening the French florist in February."

The whole class was confused. Only a few students sang that last line. Unfortunately, one of them was Zoey Cullen, who sings like a dead cow. I think she made the lights flicker, it was so bad.

Mrs. Funderbunk wretched and seemingly threw up in her mouth, before turning her back to us to compose herself. After a moment, she turned back toward us and forced a smile. "I've heard enough. How many are thinking about trying out for the holiday musical?"

A few eager participants, plus a few unsure of what others might think, raised their hands. Nobody in my row responded.

Mrs. Funderbunk pursed her lips. "Umm, yes, that's terrible." She pointed to Mark Jensen. "Mark, raise your hand," and then to me. "Austin, Sophie, you too." I looked around and then did as I was told. Sophie smiled. Mrs. Funderbunk looked at Zoey who was bouncing up and down with her hand in the air. "Zoey?"

"Yes?" she asked eagerly.

Mrs. Funderbunk said shortly. "Hand down."

Zoey kept her hand up tentatively while her face nearly fell to the floor. "Hand down? I...don't understand."

"Yes, hand down." Zoey's hand fell further. "There you go. Put it in your pocket. Good girl. Right where it should be." Zoey looked to be on the verge of tears. "I have the role of a lifetime already picked out for you."

Zoey's smile returned. "What is it?"

Mrs. Funderbunk asked, "How good are you at flipping light switches?"

Zoey scratched her head. "Umm, pretty good, I guess."

"You have ten years of experience. I'd say you're an expert. We need your talent on the crew!"

Zoey shrugged and unconvinced said, "Okay."

Mrs. Funderbunk looked around at the rest of us. "I feel really good about that. Now, how many rappers do we have? Santukkah! has a thrilling, beat-bopping, rap medley."

Nobody responded. I didn't know much about writing rap songs, but based on her description, I was concerned. She shook her head, disappointed. "That is something we shall have to remedy if Santukkah! is going to smash every Broadway record. In the meantime, let's begin our vocal training. Let's do the scales, starting in Middle C."

Zoey raised her hand. Mrs. Funderbunk eyed her curiously. "I thought we discussed the hand-raising issue already?"

"Yes, but I don't know what Middle C is."

"The rest of us already know that, dear. Let us begin!"

Over the next half hour, we went through every strange singing exercise ever devised. Mercifully, the bell eventually rang. I headed for the exit with Sophie and Ben when Mrs. Funderbunk caught my eye.

"Austin, may I have a moment of your time?" she asked.

I looked at Sophie and shrugged. She smiled and said, "Don't worry. I'll see you in science."

"Ok. See you then." I turned to look up at Mrs. Funderbunk.

She was beaming. "Young love."

I smiled sheepishly. "How can you tell?"

"I can spot it anywhere. As a playwright, I am a student of the human condition. Your chemistry reminds me of none other than Romeo and Juliet!" she said with gusto.

My mom is a bit of a Shakespeare buff, so although I'd never read any, I knew a little bit about some of the classics. I looked at Mrs. Funderbunk and frowned. "Wasn't Romeo and Juliet a tragedy? Didn't they both end up dead?"

"Oh, yes. You are quite correct, but before that, it was a love for the ages. Five glorious days of love. Well, four. The fifth day is a bit of a downer."

Five days? I wasn't sure what to make of that. Sophie and I at least had them beat on time. After a moment of confusion, I thought it best to change subjects. "What did you want to speak to me about, Mrs. Funderbunk?"

"Ahh, yes! I wanted to tell you that I think you have a lovely voice. I truly want you to try out for the holiday pageant. What do you say? You'll do it. I know you will," she said, seemingly trying to convince herself instead of me.

I shrugged. I liked to sing, but I never really thought

about doing it in front of other people. "I don't know if that's really my thing."

Mrs. Funderbunk waved her hand at me. "Oh, nonsense. I have a great eye for musical talent. I think you could be the lead."

My ears perked up. "Really?"

"Really. And Santukkah! is bound to be a classic. One for the ages." I wasn't convinced that Santukkah! had Romeo and Juliet type potential, except maybe the tragic end, nor was I sure that I was lead material. My mother always tells me that I have a voice of an angel, but I thought I might be better suited for the crew. I was an awesome light switch flipper. I nail it every time.

"Why don't you think it over? There's still some time before auditions."

"Okay. I can do that."

"Wonderful!"

"I should get going," I said with a smile.

"Have a great rest of the day, my little star!" Mrs. Funderbunk looked at me like I was the kid she never had.

I hustled off to class and then spent the rest of the day thinking about what she had said. I flip flopped back and forth, but I was starting to lean more and more toward excitement. Could I really be the lead? The star?

But then I got on the bus. As we bounced our way home, Ben peed on my parade when he asked, "You're going to sing in front of the whole school?"

"Shhh," I whispered. I was embarrassed he said it loud enough for everyone around us to hear. Sammie glanced over from the seat next to us. I wasn't sure I even wanted her to know and she was one of my closest friends since we were two years old.

Ben leaned in and whispered, "If you're worried about

people knowing that you *might* sing, how nervous do you think you'll be when you actually sing in... front...of...everyone?" he paused between each word for effect.

I thought about it for a minute. He kind of had a point. I bit my lip. "I don't know. Maybe you're right." Flipping light switches had a lot less reputational risk.

I sat in silence for most of the rest of the trip home. My thoughts bounced back and forth between fantasizing about performing as the lead and all the applause that goes along with it and nearly throwing up, worried that my knees would knock, my voice would crack, or I would fall off the stage and then serenade the stunned crowd with a theatre-rattling fart.

I zombied my way through dinner, eating like a slob and grunting when spoken to. I was still mad at everyone. I wasn't sure why, but it felt right. I guess I was just angry at the situation and I took it out on them.

I mumbled with my last bite of mashed potatoes in my mouth, "Mah I ble exclused?" I didn't wait for an answer. I slid out from my seat and dropped my plate in the sink with a clank. I avoided eye contact with them all and headed down the hall toward my bedroom.

I heard my dad whisper, "I got this, honey."

I thought about closing and locking the door before he caught up to me, but talking to my dad usually feels better, so I just left it open.

My dad followed me into my room and closed the door behind us. I plopped onto my bed and put my head under my pillow.

I bounced as my dad sat down on the edge of my bed. "What's going on, buddy boy?"

"Nothing," my muffled voice responded.

"You're the genius, but there definitely seems like there's

something." He paused for a moment and then continued, "Are you maybe a little bit jealous of Derek?"

"I just don't understand why everyone makes such a big deal over him all the time."

"Everyone makes such a big deal over you, too. They can't believe how smart you are and how well you do in school."

"Nobody wants to be a nerd, Dad," I said, frustrated.

"You're not a nerd."

"I am, too. And it just bugs me that I'm not treated the same as someone who can run fast with a football."

"I know, it's not fair. If you could get recognition for something else, what would it be?"

I perked up a little bit. "Mrs. Funderbunk says I could be the lead in the sixth-grade holiday musical."

"That's great news. Is that something you want?"

"I don't know. I do like to sing."

"You get that from me," he said proudly. I didn't want to break his heart, but he was not good. At all. He continued, "But?"

"But I'm afraid." I continued to hold the pillow over my head. It was easier to talk about it if I wasn't looking at my dad.

"Of what?"

"Of what everyone thinks. That I might mess up, you know, fall of the stage, poop in my pants, or maybe my pants might even fall off during a solo or something."

My dad laughed. "Performing is difficult, whether it's sports, singing, acting, giving presentations. That's why you prepare. Everyone gets nervous. You think your brother never got nervous before a big game?"

"Yes."

"Let me tell you something. He almost hurled before his

first start against Bayville," my dad said. I filed that one away for the future. My brother makes few mistakes. You need to capitalize when you get the opportunity.

"I just want to be good at something besides school and video games."

"Look, we all have different gifts and challenges," my dad said. "Being a middle school football star is a lot less important than getting straight A's like you do. Well, except for gym."

I let out a little laugh.

"Comparing yourself to someone else is a losing battle. You just can't worry about what other people do or what they're good at. Just be the best you. Can you do that?"

"Maybe," I whispered. I wasn't willing to commit to anything. I still felt like garbage and the next day just added to the smelly pile of it.

～

I sat in music class with Sophie and Ben at my sides. Mrs. Funderbunk stood in front of the class in a black sequined dress that was much more appropriate for the Tony Awards than for middle school music class. Still, she looked pretty as she addressed us, "Mrs. Funderbunk would like to go over some housekeeping items to start class. First, we will be adding a new student to our roster starting today. Mrs. Funderbunk expects you will give him a warm Gopher greeting. He's entirely new to the school. My assumption is that he is on his way now, probably just a minute late, learning his way around. Second, Austin will hand out a sign-up sheet for the smash hit, Santukkah!, should you choose to audition." Mrs. Funderbunk looked at Zoey. "Or join the crew." She waved me up to the front of the class.

I stood up and slid in front of Ben and walked up to Mrs. Funderbunk, unsure of why she chose me instead of the ten kids who were closer to her. I grabbed the stack of papers and started handing them out. She continued, "Austin, take one for yourself. He will, of course, be auditioning as he is an amazing talent."

I will? I told her I would think about it. That's it. I was a little embarrassed, but I liked it a little, too. I looked at Sophie and Ben and shrugged, my cheeks blushing a bit. As I made my way toward the students by the door, my ear caught a boy's voice singing in the hallway. I stopped in my tracks, listening. It was mesmerizing. Before I could snap myself out of it, Mrs. Funderbunk did it for me.

"Outta my way, boy!" Mrs. Funderbunk screamed as she blasted me with a stiff arm straight out of the Super Bowl. Mr. Muscalini would've been proud. Of her. Certainly not of me. I spun around with such force that I got dizzy and fell to the floor with a thump and a grunt. I was at least thankful I didn't fart on impact.

Mrs. Funderbunk disappeared out of the classroom in a cloud of dust bunnies. The entire class sat in shocked silence. Everybody looked around at each other, expecting someone else to have the answer. Kind of like on testing days. Sobs echoed from the hallway, as Marcus Judd helped me to my feet. No one appeared to have any idea about what was going on.

After the strangest moment of my life, well, except for the time I kept waking up dressed as Little Bo Peep (a story for another time), Mrs. Funderbunk returned with her arm wrapped around a tall, muscular boy, with blond hair. He looked like he just came from a photo shoot for Cool Kid magazine. Morgan Parish gasped while the rest of the class just stared, myself included, not sure what to make of Mrs. Funderbunk's abrupt exit and return.

Mrs. Funderbunk wiped her puffy eyes. "It's okay, children. These are tears of joy." She took a deep breath and continued, "Mrs. Funderbunk has been waiting for this her whole life. Allow me to introduce you to Cherry Avenue's newest star! Mrs. Funderbunk presents, Randy Warblemacher!"

Most of the girls just giggled. Some clapped. Even some of the dudes joined in. Randy flashed a Hollywood smile and waved to the girls like this monstrosity was totally normal. Maybe it was because of where he came from. I stood there, not really sure of what to do.

Mrs. Funderbunk looked at me with disappointment. "Sit down, Austin."

"But I haven't finished handing out all the forms."

She grabbed the forms from my hand and said, "Yes, you have, my dear."

My face started to redden. I couldn't believe she would toss me aside so quickly. Yesterday- actually two minutes ago, I was her budding star. Now, I was being tossed aside. I grabbed the corner of a signup sheet from the pile in Mrs. Funderbunk's hand and tugged one out. She didn't fight it, but she didn't make it easy, either. I folded it up and slipped it into my pocket, as I slinked back to my seat. I stewed there for the rest of the class, if you want to call it that. We basically, just observed a private lesson with Randy.

I walked into science class, excited to get some Sophie time. My face dropped when I saw the familiar blond hair of the Golden Child, Randy Warblemacher. I didn't even know the kid and I already didn't like him. At least he was partnered with someone besides me or Sophie.

Sophie smiled and said, "Hey, there."

I stared at Randy, barely listening to Sophie. "Hey," I said, absentmindedly.

"You okay?"

I snapped out of it. "Yeah, well, kinda. I felt pretty stupid in music, though."

"Yeah, she wasn't very nice to you. It doesn't matter. You're a great singer."

"Thanks," I said as the bell rang.

Mr. Gifford stood up from his desk. "Okay, we're going to do something really fun today. We're going to take our eight lab teams and have a little competition. Today is one of the best days of the year." I looked over at Randy. I normally didn't disagree with Mr. Gifford, but he was flat-out wrong. Regardless, he continued with his best, but not good enough announcer voice, "Today is air balloon racing day!"

The class oohed and aahed. Mr. Gifford smiled and said,

"Grab your kits. You'll design and make race cars, test them, and then we'll race!"

I looked over at Randy and chuckled to myself. He might best me in singing, but he was about to get put in his place. I was pumped, particularly since his partner was Ditzy Dayna Jeffries, who was going to do nothing but stare at him, twirl her hair, and giggle. My science vibe was running hot as I fantasized about crushing Randy. "You're goin' down, Candy Pants," I said.

"What?" Sophie asked.

I didn't realize I trash talked Randy out loud. "I, umm, nothing." It was best not to try to explain.

I regrouped, ready to take on the project in front of us. Sophie and I focused on creating the perfect balance of aerodynamics, height, and weight. Our race car had to be light enough that the balloon would blast it through the finish line, but big enough to hold a fully-expanded balloon. We only had fifteen minutes to design, assemble, and test it before we won the race. I don't lose in science. It's pretty much an established law of the universe, like gravity.

Sophie and I worked out a quick sketch and a plan, and got to work. As we mixed and matched wheels and other parts, Mr. Gifford wandered around the room, assessing and commenting on everyone's projects. "Nice work," I heard Mr. Gifford say.

I looked up, smiled, and said, "Thank-" before realizing he wasn't talking to me. He stood in front of Randy's table, studying his race car. "Impressive aerodynamics, Aus-er, Mr. Warblemacher." He laughed. "I almost called you Austin." Oh, not you, too, Mr. Gifford. At least he didn't cry. Regardless, I felt like poop.

"Did you say something?" Sophie asked, while still examining our car's chassis.

"No, well, yes. Don't worry about it," I said. I took a deep breath and refocused on my propulsion design.

After a few more minutes, Mr. Gifford said, "Five more minutes." He walked up to the board and started drawing a bracket like the NCAA basketball tournament, four student groups on each side. Whoever won three races in a row would win the competition. And by whoever, I meant me and Sophie.

The first race was about to start. Mr. Gifford laid out masking tape on both ends of the classroom as the start and finish lines. Sophie and I lined up against Kami Rahm and Amanda Bradley. I took one look at their racer and knew we would win. I blew up the balloon and handed it to Sophie. "You want to let her go?"

Sophie looked at me uncertain. "Okay. If you want me to."

Sophie held our racer next to Kami. Mr. Gifford stood across the room at the finish line. "On your mark. Get set. Go."

The cars took off, the balloons fizzling and propelling the cars forward. Ours had a solid track to the finish line, taking off quickly. The class cheered. Team Kami and Amanda veered off the path and smashed into a lab table. The class groaned while the balloon leaked out the last of its air in a squeak. One race down. Two to go.

Next up was Bryce Simon and Ava Sasser against Ditzy Dayna and Randy Warblemacher. Ava was the president of the robotics club. Nighty night, Randy. I nearly started laughing out loud.

Randy placed his car down next to Ava. She looked up at Randy and smirked. Both cars looked pretty good. We would beat either of them, but this was going to be a decent race.

Mr. Gifford held up his hand and said, "Ready. Set. Go!"

The cars took off across the floor, neck and neck. Both balloons emptied, propelling the cars forward. The class cheered as Mr. Gifford yelled, "It's gonna be a photo finish!" Randy and Dayna's car inched out their competition for the victory.

"We have a winner! Ditzy, er, Dayna and the newcomer, Randy take the round!"

"Did you see that?" Kami Rahm asked me.

"Yeah," I grumbled. "It was pretty okay."

"Pretty okay? It was awesome!"

Amanda Bradley chimed in with a whisper, "He's smart and hot? This is too good to be true." It was, but not everybody saw it.

Sophie and I took down Jason Tannen and Mary Casey with ease and were set to meet Ditzy Dayna and Randy in the finals.

I blew up the balloon and set it in place on our car. Sophie said, "You do this one. I don't want you blaming me if we lose." She smiled.

"We're not gonna lose," I said.

Randy placed his car on the line and said, "I wouldn't be too sure. I don't lose. So that means you're about to, loser."

I took a deep breath. I looked over at Randy. "Are you wearing cologne?"

"That's what men do," he said, way too confidently. "Maybe you'll grow up one day enough to handle cologne. Until then I hear Arianna Grande has a new perfume that would smell good on you. I think it has lavender in it."

"Whatever," I said. I really had nothing better to say.

I heard Mary Casey whisper behind me, "Do you really think he can beat Austin?"

I'd been crushing science for years. Did they really think

one shiny, new kid was going to stop me? Mr. Gifford held up his hand and said, "Ready. Set. Go!" He caught me by surprise. I let our hot rod loose.

Our cars took off across the floor to screams. I smiled as I watched our car take a slim lead. I heard Sophie yell, "Go! Go! Go!" It helped as we gained more ground.

I watched, breathless, as the balloons emptied. The cars continued to roll toward the finish line. My eyes widened as Randy's car gained on ours. The hot rod slowed faster than in the last race. My mouth dropped open as Randy's car surged past ours. The crowd erupted in cheers and gasps.

I stood up, my shoulders slumping. I was shocked. Time slowed down. Sophie rubbed my shoulder and said, "Don't worry. It's not a big deal."

I stared at her in disbelief. Not a big deal? The only thing that I loved more than science was my brother's failures and those were few and far between. My whole world had been turned upside down and shaken like one of those snow globe things that my mother loves so much. Except for the fake little snow, Randy sprinkled a whole bunch of poop in there.

I watched the celebration. Randy looked at me as everyone congratulated him. He smiled and mouthed the word, "Loser." I continued to stare at him. He mouthed, "You stink. I'll buy you some perfume."

I THINK about my life in two periods of time: Before Randy (B.R.) and After Randy (A.R.). Day two A.R. was no better than day one. I woke up with my first zit ever and it was a beast. I thought it might beat me up and take my lunch money.

Some would look at Randy's arrival and the transformation of my sweet, baby skin to The Creature and say, "It's just a coincidence." Me? I don't believe in them. I blame it all on Randy. And it seemed like everywhere I turned, there he was.

I sat in music class, waiting for Sophie and Ben to show up. I looked up as someone walked in. My heart dropped. It was Randy. He looked at me, confused. "What's your name again? Davenfart, is it?" He plopped into a seat in the front row.

"Yeah, funny. You really know how to fit in around here."

Randy turned around and looked at me. "I don't need to fit in, little man. People need to fit in with me." He looked me up and down and then almost puked. "Ugh, dude. What's that thing on your face? Is it alive?"

I covered my zit and search his face for any imperfection I could find, but I came up empty. He had the skin of a porcelain doll. Randy laughed and turned back around as Mrs. Funderbunk walked in with a few students behind her. I shook my head, muttering under my breath. He was the blond version of Derek. I tried to look on the bright side. At least Randy didn't have a butt chin.

I saw Sophie in the atrium after school. She walked up to me with a smile and said, "Hey!"

I smiled. "Hey."

"What's the matter?" Sophie asked.

I shrugged.

"You haven't been yourself lately."

I shrugged again. I didn't want to tell her the truth. That I didn't feel like I was good enough. I already thought she was too good for me. I didn't want her to start thinking it. "I guess I've just been a little nervous trying to figure out whether or not to try out for the holiday musical." That wasn't all of it, but it was all I felt like talking about.

"I think you could be really good. What part are you thinking about?"

"The lead," I said.

"Oh," she whispered.

"What's the matter?" I asked.

"I thought you knew Randy was going to get that."

"Thanks for your support. I'm glad you have my back." This Randy kid was starting to get on my nerves. Stomping on them was more like it.

The next morning, I had the pleasure of bumping into Randy again, this time on the way to my locker before school started. I saw him out of the corner of my eye and tried to walk by unnoticed, but Randy spotted me.

"Hey Davenfart, my girlfriend told me that *you're* trying out for the lead in the musical?" Randy laughed. He had a girlfriend already? Geez, man. This kid was good.

"I haven't decided," I lied. "Why do you care what I do, anyway?" I asked.

"I don't. You're not going to get the part. I'd just hate to see you embarrass yourself."

"I doubt that."

He shrugged. "Yeah, you're right. I'd love to see you embarrass yourself."

I was about to respond, but then I realized that there were only two people who knew about what I wanted to do in the musical, Ben and Sophie. "Who even told you that?"

"I told you, my girlfriend. Her name is Sophie. I heard you used to date her."

Used to? I felt sick.

"Adiós, loser." Randy chuckled to himself and walked away.

I zombie-walked over to my locker. My hands were shaking so much that I had to try my combo three times before I got it open.

Sophie walked up to me and smiled. She looked at me and frowned. "What's the matter now?"

"Everything." I slammed my books into the back of the locker. I think I might've dented it.

"Can you be more specific?"

"No," I spat.

"Okay...Are you mad at me?" she asked, confused.

"You're a smart girl. I knew you'd figure it out." I stuffed my backpack into my locker and slammed it shut.

"And?"

I turned to face her. "If you don't want to be my girlfriend, I wish you would've told me instead of having to hear it from Randy. Oh, and thanks for telling him I was trying out for the lead."

"I never said I didn't want to be your girlfriend, but with your attitude..."

"What?" So he just made it up?"

"Yes."

"And what about the musical?"

"I did tell him that. I'm sorry."

"I can't believe you did that." I stared at the floor, my face reddening.

"I wasn't thinking."

"No, no you weren't. Now he's taunting me."

"Oh, I'm sure you're exaggerating. He's nice."

"To you, maybe. He thinks you're dating. To me, he's a

jerkwad." I didn't know if that was even a word, but I thought it sounded good.

"I gotta go," Sophie said, annoyed.

I watched her walk off in a huff.

Science was not any better. Saustin (our couple name) was struggling. Tension was running higher than when we pick teams in gym class. For a nerd that's some serious tension. Sophie walked in, her lips pursed. She dropped her binder on the lab table and slid into her seat.

"Hey," she said, less than enthused.

"Hey," I said, trying to be a little more upbeat than the last time we spoke.

Mr. Gifford began his lecture before we could really talk about anything. He explained our lab project. We were still working on gases with balloons. I wondered if Mr. Gifford had a second job as a clown making balloon animals. He had so many of them.

I read some additional instructions on the board and said, "There are two parts. Let's work on the first one together."

Sophie frowned and said, "It probably would be easier for each of us to work separately and then add the pieces together."

"Okay," I said, tentatively. Did she not want to work with me? We were Saustin. What was happening? I took a deep breath and started working on my part.

After a few moments, I looked over at Sophie. "I can't seem to get it right," I whispered.

Sophie looked over at Randy and nodded. "Take a look and see what Randy's doing. He seems to have it down."

I glared at Sophie, squinting my eyes so much that I almost couldn't see her. "I don't need Randy's help in science, thank you very much. And are you trying to get me mad?"

"It's not a big deal to get things wrong once and a while."

"I didn't get anything wrong," I snapped. "It's an experiment. You have to try different things before you find what works." I shook my head like she just didn't understand.

She huffed, grabbed her text book, and started flipping through it.

I wasn't sure if I was going to lose her or not. I liked her a lot. She was kind, smart, and beautiful. There were fifty kids cooler than me that she could date, maybe a hundred. And then there was Candy Pants, Randy. It was becoming more and more likely that my first girlfriend was going to become my first ex-girlfriend, and I didn't know how to stop that from happening.

I went back to my project and eventually worked it out. While I was putting the finishing touches on it, deep in concentration, Gary Larkin took his full balloon and rubbed it on the top of my head before I could get out of the way. The static electricity caused my hair to stand on end like I had just stuck my finger in the electrical socket. The whole class laughed.

Mr. Gifford chuckled to himself. His bald head reflected the overhead lights. "To be young again," he sighed. "Finish up. Only a few minutes left."

Once it was quiet again, I blew up my balloon, snuck up behind Gary and put the opening near his ear. I flattened and stretched the neck of the balloon, squeaking it in his ear like a long, high-pitched fart. I sang, "Beans, beans, make you fart..." I laughed as he swatted my hand away. The balloon got away from me. The air fizzled out of it and landed on Sophie's notebook. She rolled her eyes.

I shrugged and then froze as Randy walked over to

Sophie, his red balloon shaped like a heart. He handed it to her and said, "Have my heart."

A few girls sighed lovingly while Ditzy Dayna giggled. Everyone else's eyes widened. Sophie took the heart and put it next to her notebook. "Thank you, Randy. That's very sweet."

I didn't know what to do. Randy eyed me on his way back to his seat and smirked.

I sat down quickly next to Sophie. "What was that about?" I whispered.

"You have eyes."

"Why didn't you tell him you had a boyfriend?"

"I didn't want to embarrass him. It's not a big deal."

"He doesn't seem to care about embarrassing anyone else." Or maybe it was just me.

"Austin, I said it wasn't a big deal."

I just shook my head, fuming.

I wasn't sure if she was lying to me or not, because later I heard her whisper to Lia Malkin, "It was kinda sweet." Uh, oh.

I needed to make Randy appear human. He was too perfect. I blew up my balloon again. I was going to try the static electricity trick that Gary did to me. Either he would look like a dork with his hair standing up or he would get angry and say something rude. Both were a win for me.

I snuck up behind Randy and rubbed the balloon on the top of his head. It didn't budge. Really? How was this possible? The dude must've spent his whole allowance on hair product. It remained stubbornly perfect, defying the laws of physics! At that moment, I knew I was doomed.

"Can I help you?" Randy said as he turned around. He smiled and whispered so no one else could hear, "Oh, it's just you, Davenfart. Did anyone ever tell you that you remind them of a gnat? Your zit is getting better, though. It's only the size of an asteroid now."

I popped my balloon out of anger as the bell rang. I walked back to my table to gather my things and Sophie was already on her way out the door, leaving me behind without even a goodbye.

Randy walked over to her, staring at the school map. I heard him say, "Hey, Sophie, can you show me where room 216 is?"

Sophie looked at me, annoyed, and then at Randy. "Yeah, I'm going that way."

Ahhhh, farts.

I DIDN'T SEE Sophie for the rest of the day. I texted her a few times and didn't get any responses. My anxiety level was rising. I was losing her. As I lay in my bed, I decided to call her. I grabbed my phone and hit the Favorites button and pressed Sophie's name. The phone rang once, twice, three times. My heart pounded harder each time. Finally, she answered with, "I have to call you back."

"Okay," I said to no one, as she had already hung up. I waited for an hour. She didn't return my call. I paced around my room, wondering if I should call her again. Maybe she forgot? Maybe she just didn't want to talk to me. Maybe she was on the other line with Randy. Maybe I was going to vomit on my bunny slippers.

My relationship with Sophie was like a fat guy wrapped in bacon on cracked ice, standing above shark-infested water. There was room for improvement. And it was all Randy Warblemacher's doing. Balancing school work, taming my beastly zit, and making things right with Sophie were testing my mettle. I couldn't believe she hadn't called me back. On the plus side, my bunny slippers made it through the night without any regurgitational splatteration.

Waiting at the bus stop the next morning, I stood with Ben and Sammie, huddled by ourselves, talking. "I mean, can you believe he did that?" I asked.

"What a jerk," Ben said, helpfully.

"But isn't he just so hot?" Sammie asked, a lot less helpful.

"Who cares what he looks like? He's mean," I said, trying not to lose my temper.

"He seems nice to me," Sammie replied. "Does he have a girlfriend?"

"Haven't you been listening to anything I've said? And

what about Derek?" Sammie had always had a crush on my brother. I didn't approve of it for her sake, but it was better than Randy. And I knew my brother didn't like her that way.

"He's okay, but Randy..."

This was worse than I thought. Beyond my wildest nightmares. If you told me Sammie would go from drooling Derek admirer to "He's okay" in two days, I would've said you should check to make sure your head is still connected to the rest of you.

My stomach felt queasy. I was afraid of what might happen with Sophie and me. We were Saustin, the cute and perhaps, unlikely couple, that everyone loved. I gave nerds everywhere hope that they, too, could find a girl they thought was out of their league. And it all was unraveling. I had to make it right, if not for myself, then for Nerd Nation.

I was pretty quiet until we made it to school. Once we got there, I stood inside the atrium, waiting for Sophie's bus to let out. I tried to shake out the jitters, which earned me some strange looks from some of my classmates. I was kind of used to it. I was half expecting Sophie and Randy to walk in together, arm in arm, with matching outfits, hair blowing in the wind, and a cute flower girl, dropping rose petals at their feet. I'm not a mean kid, but if that would've happened, I probably would've tripped her. The flower girl, not Sophie. I was that out of sorts. Thankfully, Sophie walked in with Ditzy Dayna and not Randy. I waved and she walked over.

I took a deep breath and said, "Hey."

"Hey," she responded.

"Late night studying last night?" I asked. I wanted to know why she didn't call me back.

"Nope."

"Did your phone die?"

"No."

"Did your grandma die?"

"What?" Sophie asked annoyed. "What kind of question is that?"

""Umm, forget it. Why didn't you call me back last night?"

"I got sidetracked. Sorry."

Sidetracked? Sorry? My poor bunny slippers almost died and all she said was, "Sorry"?

From there, the day just got better. It was a gym day. I walked onto the basketball court and nearly cried. Randy Warblemacher stood at center court, talking animatedly with Mr. Muscalini. Randy in science was one thing. That was when I was at my best. Randy in my gym class? I was downright doomed in his domain.

Ben said something, but it didn't compute. My head was swirling with unhelpful thoughts, mainly wondering if Randy was somehow capable of picking me up and dunking me into the basketball hoop, headfirst.

Mr. Muscalini stepped toward the class and blew his whistle. "Okay, I'm going to break you up into groups so you can apply the skills we've been learning and play half-court scrimmages." You can guess who was in my group, Randy "LeBron James" Warblemacher, ready to take his basketball talents to my face.

Randy nodded to me as I stood with Ben, Duncan Strauss, and Zack Franklin. I thought he was somehow showing some common decency and sportsmanship until he leaned into me and whispered, "I'm going to crush you, Davenfart."

"We'll see about that," I said, fully knowing that I would not be seeing anything about that.

Nobody wanted to guard Randy. I certainly wasn't going to do it. I walked over to Scottie Washington, a student with my similar lack of talent. Us nerds might go head to head in science, math, and English class, but in gym, we stick together. I leaned in and whispered, "You know the routine."

Scottie did not know the routine. He looked white as a ghost. "Dude, I can't play basketball."

"Here's what we do. We guard each other. Just follow me around when we have the ball and I'll follow you when your team does. Move away from the ball and don't look at whoever has it. Okay?"

"Okay," he said, shakily.

"Ladies first," I heard Randy say and then felt the ball whip me in the kidney. Some of the kids laughed. I rubbed my side and then grabbed the ball. I knew enough about playing hoops from Derek. I passed it in to Duncan and ran in the opposite direction, according to the nerd hoops rules I had just laid out to Scottie.

Randy took over the game immediately. He swatted the ball away from Duncan, turned around, and drove to the hoop, scoring with a layup. "Try to keep up, guys. I'm bored already," Randy taunted us.

It was Randy versus everyone else. Sometimes even his own team. He stole it from Jimmy Bambino four times and he was the second-best player on Randy's team. He drained shot after shot, skying over all of us on one play and then launching fade-away jump shots on the next. He also set the record for elbows. I took at least six to the ribs and back and that was just after Mr. Muscalini blew the whistle. I can't even count how many I took in the actual game.

We didn't know how to stop him. He was even better than Derek. And I had given up playing against Derek years ago. He was so obnoxious that I decided to break the nerd rule and actually try to help my team play defense to stop the jerk. But the only defensive play that ever worked for me back then was what I call, the Five-Toe Flank. Others might call it a trip.

On the next play, Randy hogged the ball once again, driving the lane with Duncan and Zack on each hip, and three of his teammates wide open at the wings. I stepped into the lane and executed a textbook Five-Toe Flank to Randy's ankle. The ball flew wide while Randy stumbled and ultimately collided with the padded gym wall. He crumpled to the ground. Duncan cheered while Zack high-fived me.

I could hear Randy whining underneath his hands, "My face...my beautiful face." That's what you get when you mix sports with a pretty boy actor. I didn't mean for him to get hurt, but after all he had done to me and everyone else, I didn't feel that bad, either. Bullies get very little sympathy from Nerd Nation.

A crowd gathered around Randy, as Mr. Muscalini stepped forward and yelled at me, "What was that, Davenport?"

I turned, not sure of what to say. "Defense, sir?"

"Step in front! Take the charge! Warblemacher- take Davenport here and run him over ten times so he learns to take a charge like a man!"

"Sir, is that necessary?" I asked, a pleading look on my face.

"Is air necessary, Davenport?" Mr. Muscalini countered.

You didn't have to be a science whiz like me to know the answer to that. "Yes, sir."

"Well, what're you waiting for?" He asked.

I shrugged. "For you to answer the question. Do I really have to get run over, risk getting concussed, to teach me to take the charge?"

"Life is about taking the charge, Davenport!"

I guessed he meant it was necessary. Randy stepped out of the crowd, a wicked smile on his face. He knocked the ball out of Marcus Judd's hand and dribbled between his legs as he walked over to me. "Time to pay, Davenfart."

⁓

RANDY GAVE ME QUITE A WHOOPING. And he thoroughly enjoyed it. Me? Not so much. I was rubbing my butt as I walked to my locker. I saw Zorch, our custodian and my friend, heading toward me, panic in his eyes. We stopped to talk. "What's the matter?" I asked.

He leaned down toward me and whispered, "Principal Buthaire is going to search your locker for evidence."

"Evidence for what?" I asked.

"The office break in. The dance. Whatever he can to get you in trouble."

"What is he looking for?"

"I don't know. A lock pick set, Computer Hacking for Dummies, a Zip drive containing fart sounds?"

"I downloaded the fart sounds right from his computer, so that shouldn't be a problem. There's nothing there." I wasn't worried, but then I remembered how I was framed for the baby powder incident. But that was from my brother. Would Principal Buthaire do the same? I looked up at Zorch and said, "Thanks. I'll go make sure it's all good."

"Okay, little buddy."

And I was off, forgetting that my butt hurt, running toward my locker. I slid to a stop in front of it, nearly bumping into my locker buddy, Just Charles. "Hey, man," I said.

"Hey," he said, happily, and then whispered, "Incoming."

I looked to my left to see Principal Buthaire staring down his nose at me with a broad grin on his face. The feeling was not mutual. "Greetings and salutations, Mr. Davenport."

"Hi, Principal Buthaire. Have a great day. I have to get to class." I didn't have any of my books, but I wasn't going to let that stop me, nor did I want to open my locker in front of him for fear that a farting machine was planted in there or something.

"Don't go anywhere just yet." Principal Buthaire snapped his fingers.

I looked around, not sure of what was going on. He turned around and looked behind me. His shoulders slumped. He shook his head as Zorch turned the corner and hurried toward us.

"You're late, Mr. Zorch," Principal Buthaire scolded.

"I'm sorry, sir. Toilet clog." He winked at me as Principal Buthaire turned to face me.

Principal Buthaire raised his hand and snapped his fingers again, ceremoniously. "Mr. Zorch, open this student's locker."

"Yes, sir," Zorch said and stepped forward. He unlocked my locker with a key and pulled it open.

"Now, search it," Principal Buthaire ordered.

Zorch checked my backpack and under a few books. He turned to Principal Buthaire and shrugged, a notebook still in his hand.

"You call that a searching?" Principal Buthaire asked, annoyed. He stepped forward, took the notebook out of Zorch's hand and tossed it over his shoulder.

"Hey," I whined and scurried to pick it up.

Principal Buthaire rifled through my locker, checking in every notebook and zippered compartment in my backpack. By the time he was done, my locker looked like a war zone. He turned to me and said, "I'm going to get you, Mr. Davenport. Don't think you've bested me today."

"I don't think that, sir."

"Good. Because you haven't." He smiled and looked at his accomplishment with pride. "We've got quite a mess here." He raised his index finger in the air and called out, "De-Tent-Shaaawn!" Principal Buthaire laughed and held out his hand to Zorch for a high-five. He reluctantly obliged. Principal Buthaire was losing it. Or perhaps already did.

"That's not fair! You just tossed my locker like a salad!"

Principal Buthaire handed me a detention slip. I took it and looked up at him, dejectedly. "I can't win."

Principal Buthaire smiled and said, "I'm glad you finally see things my way." He looked at Mr. Zorch and said, "Do you think they have fingerprint kits on Amazon?" Uh, oh. My prints were probably all over his office from when I broke into the Butt Crack. Or so the rumor has it.

"I don't know, sir."

"Well, I would suggest you find out." Principal Buthaire looked at me and said, "I'm glad we've had this little meeting. Now run along."

5

I couldn't wait for school to end. I had quite the day. Plus, I needed to find Zorch. I wasn't sure if Zorch was a Prime member or not, but I figured that worst case, I had at least two days before he started collecting fingerprints, but the sooner the better.

And then things got worse. As I sat, staring at the clock in eighth period, the speaker crackled and the evil voice of Principal Buthaire echoed throughout our class, "We interrupt this programming to bring you this important message...our security team will be searching backpacks, handbags, briefcases, suitcases, man bags, and fanny packs for all non-educational items. They are strictly forbidden and will be confiscated immediately and never returned." The speaker cut off in the middle of his evil cackle.

Luke Hill turned to me and said, "What the heck is a fanny pack?"

I just shrugged. I think he missed the main idea. Cherry Avenue Middle School Prison was going to Maximum Lockdown Status. I contemplated breaking out my prison costume again.

The bell rang and I moped out of class, keeping an eye out for Zorch as I headed for the bus. Thankfully, I ran into him outside on the sidewalk.

He walked up to me shaking his head. "I'm sorry, Austin. He's my boss."

"I know. It's not your fault. You know, I was thinking," I said, hand on my chin. "You always do such a nice job cleaning the windows. I wonder if The Butt Crack, er, Principal Buthaire's office has been cleaned since the break in."

Zorch cracked a smile, no pun intended (well, maybe a little). He shook his head. "No, I think those windows are overdue."

I smiled. "I'm sure he would love a crystal-clear view of the courtyard. You might want to focus a lot of time on the area where one might place their hand to slide the window open from the outside."

"I will make sure it sparkles."

"Thanks! Gotta catch my ride." I hustled off, barely squeezing through the closing bus doors. Miss Alyssa is a big stickler to the schedule. Had I been trapped half in and half out of the bus, I think she still would've left.

After I finished my homework, I sat on the couch icing my butt and singing. I was perhaps delirious from getting run over by Randy so many head-rattling times. I played the drums on my knees while I sang, "Randy...you broke my butt, but not my spirit. If you're anti-Randy, let me hear it. Yeah, yeah, yeah. Randy...Warblemacher, I wanna slam your face inside a locker. I wished you looked just like Chewbacca. Yeah, yeah, yeaheheaaa!" I ended on a high note and the crowd went nuts. "Thank you and good night, Cherry Avenue!"

Pretty good, right? Who knows? I thought that if science didn't work out, maybe I could be the next breakout singer-songwriter. Anyway, my dad walked in, nodding his head. "Groovy tunes, dude," which basically crushed my brief and fragile singer-songwriter dream.

"What?" I asked.

"Your singing. Sounds good."

"Oh, that. Just messing around. But it's not any good."

"Yes, it is. What were you singing, though? It sounded a little dark."

"I have a new nemesis," I said, nonchalantly. "He broke my butt in gym and is trying to steal my girlfriend. You know, normal kid stuff."

My dad sat down on the couch, bouncing me up. I winced in pain. "He really did break your butt. What's going on with this kid?"

"I don't know. We both want the same girl, the same part in the holiday musical."

"What do you think will happen?"

"He's probably going to win both," said, the energy draining from my body with each word.

"He's just great at everything. Even better than Derek. He's even a bigger jerk than Derek."

He held in a chuckle. "Listen to me," my dad said calmly, "You'll always have problems, always feel that you are not enough when you compare yourself to others. Be the best you. If he's better, so be it."

I sighed and whined, "But he'll be so annoying..."

"It's a team effort. There have to be other parts."

"But I want the lead."

"Why?"

"Because I want to beat him and because I want people to cheer me."

"Do it because you love to perform."

"I love to sing. When I was ten, I wanted to be a singer-songwriter."

"You're still ten."

"I've matured a lot since then. I guess I feel older."

My dad laughed, "Did you ever hear the saying, 'there are no small parts, only small actors?'"

"Yes, but I have no idea what that means."

"It means that there are only parts in a play. There are no big ones, leads, or little ones. And they each deserve the actor's best effort and attention. Any actor who doesn't give his or her best because they feel the part isn't big enough for their talent isn't doing the role or their teammates justice."

"I think I understand," I said. "Is there a way I can play a lesser role and still crush Randy?"

"I'm not sure you understand," my dad said through laughter. "Go for the lead. If you get it, great. If you don't, give whatever part you get your best. It doesn't matter what Randy does. There are no individual winners. Only the acting team wins or loses."

"I'm pretty certain that's not how he'll see it and I will have to hear it every day until eternity is over."

My dad laughed. "Well, that's not that long, so I'm sure you can handle it."

I decided I was going to go out for the lead and crush Randy in the process. It might not have been exactly what my father told me to do, but it was what I felt in my heart. I spent the rest of the night binge watching every audition from every TV show I could get my hands on: American Idol, America's Got Talent, and The Voice. I listened to all of the judges' commentary and critiques. I was so confused. But I was motivated. I had a dream. No. A goal. And it was going to be mine and not butt-breaking Randy's.

6

The next the morning, I stood at the bus stop in my normal huddle. I looked at Ben and shook my head, "Dude, my butt hurts so bad."

"Yeah, well, your face hurts me."

"Very funny. In other news, I've fully decided to go out for the lead in Santukkah! I'm going to crush Randy Warblemacher teeny, tiny head in my locker." I guess the song was still stuck in my own head.

"Dude, that's harsh. But I'm in on the musical, too. I've got an excellent singing voice. I'm sure there's an important role for someone with my talents." I wasn't convinced of that, but the more the merrier.

"I'm gonna join the crew," Sammie chimed in.

"Really? Why?" I asked. I shouldn't have.

"No reason," she whispered, her face flushing pink.

"Awww, really? Randy?" Ugh.

"I didn't say that," Sammie said.

"You didn't have to," Ben laughed.

I shook my head as the bus approached. It was a quiet ride. I was excited about trying out for the musical, until we arrived at prison five minutes early. Who doesn't love to spend more time than they have to at school? I frowned as I saw kids lined up outside, waiting to get through the main entrance.

"What the heck?" I said to no one in particular.

"Bag checks. Remember?" Ben responded.

"Welcome to Cherry Avenue, where there ain't no cherries and there ain't no gophers."

"What does that even mean?" Sammie asked.

"Why does everybody expect me to have all the answers?" I asked the sky.

We waited our turn to get our bags searched like little untrustworthy criminals. After another few minutes, we got to the security table. I was probably going to be late for Advisory. I'm sure Principal Buthaire was waiting for me inside with a detention slip.

The burly security guard standing in front of me eyed me suspiciously. I placed my backpack on the table and said, "You can take my math book, if you want it."

The security guard frowned and said, "You sayin' I'm stupid?"

"Umm, no. Just a joke about not liking math."

"Bad joke."

"I see that now."

The guard finished checking my bag and pushed it toward me. "I'm watching you."

I slung my backpack on my shoulder. "I'm used to that."

I walked in to school to see Sophie waiting for me across the atrium. That was a good sign. I was excited to tell her I was trying out for the lead. I didn't care if she thought Randy would beat me out for the part. She folded up a piece of paper and slipped it into her bag, and then waved to me with a smile.

"What were you reading? I asked out of curiosity.

"A note," she said, simply.

"From who?" I asked, a little less curiously.

"From whom," she corrected me. Oh, God. That's something Randy would say. Why was she acting like him?

"From whom?" I asked.

"It's from Randy."

My heart dropped. I didn't know how to proceed. "What? Why?" I asked nervously, "Can I read it?"

"No."

"Why not?"

"It's for me. It's private."

I shifted on my feet back and forth. "But you're my girlfriend and he's trying to take you from me," I said, my voice rising.

Sophie looked around and whispered firmly, "If he wanted you to read it, he would've given you a copy."

I nodded my head slowly, my pulse and anger rising quickly.

"I don't want you talking to him," I said.

"You can't tell me who to talk to," she said, angrily.

"Then don't talk to jerks."

"I just said not to tell me who to talk to!"

"I wasn't telling you who not to talk to. I was saying that if you didn't talk to jerks, I wouldn't have to tell you who not to talk to."

Sophie huffed, "I'm so confused!" She turned and stormed off.

"Me, too!" I yelled as she walked away.

The more I thought about everything happening with Sophie, the more motivated I became to crush Randy in the musical auditions. I didn't know how I would do it, but I was going to find a way. I also had to figure out how to keep the two of them from spending any time together.

When it was time for music class, I weaved through the crowds like a running back heading for a touchdown. Well, if the running back couldn't actually run and had no athletic talent whatsoever. I slid into the class. It was basically empty except for Randy, Skylar Sparks, and Kimmy Fields. I wasn't happy to see Randy, but as long as Sophie wasn't there talking to him, I could handle whatever he threw at me.

Randy sipped from a mug and then sang, "How, now, brown cow."

Kimmy Fields slid over a few seats closer to Randy. She twirled her hair and smiled. The reflection of the light off of her braces nearly blinded me.

Kimmy asked Randy, "So, whatcha drinkin'?"

Randy said, "It's a mixture of tea and honey to protect my voice."

I shook my head. What an idiot. The room was filling up quickly. Ben and Sophie walked in together and sat in their usual places.

I leaned over to Sophie and said, "I know you don't believe I can do it, but I wanted you to know that I am trying out for the lead."

"Good for you," she said, quietly. "I'm trying out, too."

"Oh, I didn't think you were interested."

"You thought wrong," Sophie said, simply.

Mrs. Funderbunk said something about the deadline for Santukkah! I didn't really hear what she said, but I already knew when it was.

We continued to whisper to each other. I asked Sophie, "Did Randy ask you to try out?"

"I talked to him about it, but he didn't ask me."

"Why didn't you talk to me about it?"

"You haven't exactly been great to talk to lately."

Ouch.

7

School was over. I was staying after for the robotics club meeting. The halls had all but emptied out, except for a few nerds and athletes. I was at my locker, packing up my bag. I looked out of the corner of my eye and saw the last person I wanted to see. Randy walked up to me slowly. I looked down to make sure my shoelaces were tied in case I needed to make a quick exit. Not that I could actually outrun him, but I would at least try and hope he slipped or something. He smiled, but it wasn't his normal 'I'm going to get you' smile. It seemed genuine. I raised an eyebrow, intrigued by the situation that was developing.

"What do you want?" I asked.

"Just to talk, dude. Really, to give you an apology." He continued to walk toward me. He carried a slip of paper in his hand.

"For what?" I felt I needed clarification. I lost track of how many apologies he owed me.

"For being mean. I said and did some things that weren't nice. I know you're not a bad kid. Being the new kid is hard."

"Being the kid that kids pick on is hard," I said. I wasn't

going to let him off easy. "You don't have to be a jerk because you're the new kid."

"I know. I'm sorry." Randy held out the piece of paper in his hand. "Here. Take this."

"What is this?" I grabbed the paper and looked at it.

"It's the audition form for the musical, Santukkah!" He gestured as if it were up on a marquee on Broadway like Mrs. Funderbunk would do.

I cracked a smile. "Thanks, but I already have one." I held it out for Randy to take it back.

"Can you just use this one? Take it as a gesture of truce, friendship even. I don't want to discourage you from trying out, even..."

"Even, what?" I thought he was going to insult me somehow.

"Even if you win the lead."

I thought about it for a moment. "Okay," I said. I folded the paper up and slipped it into my front pocket. I held out my hand for a shake. I didn't want to be friends with Randy, but I didn't want to be enemies, either. It wasn't working all that well for me.

He grabbed my hand and shook it. "May the best man

win the lead."

I smiled. Oh, I intend to, Mr. Warblemacher.

On my way to robotics, I saw Mrs. Funderbunk talking to a teacher I didn't know. As I walked by, I smiled and said, "Hi, Mrs. Funderbunk!"

Mrs. Funderbunk looked at me and her face dropped. "Hello, Mr. Davenport," she said, her lips pursed. She seemed upset. She was a little bit of a wacko, so I didn't pay it any mind as I continued to the club.

After robotics club was over, I made my way out to the parking lot, so my mom could pick Ben and me up. We walked through the atrium together. Ben nodded to a security camera seemingly tracking us across the room.

Ben said, "Say cheese."

"Huh?" I asked.

"Smile for the camera. Looks like they're fully operational again," Ben said, shaking his head.

"Ugh. Clear your afternoons. Detentions are about to soar again. My next robotics club meeting will be in high school. I knew it was coming, but still..." The idea of being watched at every turn was so frustrating.

When we got to the exit, I was so angry that I pushed the door open with as much force as I possibly could. I was probably going to get detention for that. The door slammed open and we walked through it.

Zorch was running over, his eyes wide. He yelled, "Whoa, whoa, whoa!" Once he realized it was us, he slowed down and the steam stopped pouring from his ears.

"Austin, my doors. Try to be more careful."

"Sorry. Just frustrated that we're being watched again."

"A lot of parents support it. They want you to be safe."

"That's not what he uses it for," I said, frustrated.

"I know. There are probably things you could do. *Somebody* already took the system down once."

I looked up at Zorch and asked, "What should we, er, that *someone* do?"

"Do what you're good at."

"Burping the alphabet?" Ben asked.

Zorch laughed. "Not what I had in mind, no. You're smart kids. You'll figure out how to get rid of the cameras."

"How am I supposed to take them out? I'm sure his computer is secure. I can't start spray painting them. Security won't let me get through with spray paint anyway."

"You're the brainiac, kid. I just work here."

My mom pulled up. I gave Zorch a high-five and said, "Adiós, Zorchacho." I hustled off with Ben at my heels.

On the way home, my brain tried to compute the problem, but I couldn't come up with anything. It was hard enough the first time and that was when Principal Buthaire didn't see it coming. I'm sure he stepped up his game in the defense department. Taking out the cameras this time was going to be a whole lot more difficult.

8

The next morning, I arrived early for music class as I did for all classes that contained both Randy and Sophie. Neither of them were there. Mrs. Funderbunk sat at her desk, reading. She glanced up as I strode across the classroom.

"Hi, Mrs. Funderbunk," I said as friendly as possible. I still wasn't sure why she was mad at me from the hallway the day before, but I wanted to leave that in the past.

"Mmm, hmm," Mrs. Funderbunk responded without looking at me.

I frowned as I searched through my backpack. I grabbed the sign-up sheet for the audition and walked over to Mrs. Funderbunk. I held it out for her. "I'm trying out for the lead in Santukkah! Here's my form."

Mrs. Funderbunk still refused to look at me. "Mrs. Funderbunk regrets to inform you that you missed the deadline. It was two days ago."

"What? What are you talking about?" I asked, my voice two octaves higher than normal. I turned the paper toward me and read the deadline. "Look at the deadline. I didn't miss anything. That's today. Please, I have to try out."

Mrs. Funderbunk looked up at the paper and squinted. "Did you fudge those dates?"

"Of course not." I looked at the paper and said, "Randy gave it to me."

"Really?"

"Yes, I swear on my Pokémon collection."

She thought about it for a moment. I held my breath. Mrs. Funderbunk said, "Okay. You can audition. They're in two days. You have to learn all of Joseph's lines and songs."

"Oh, that's no problem. No problem at all," I said, excitedly. "Did I really miss the deadline?"

"You did. That Randy," she said, shaking her head.

"I know, right? I mean, how could he do that to me?"

"I can't believe him," she said, but I was confused, because she seemed happy while I was mad.

"I don't understand," I said.

Mrs. Funderbunk smiled and said, "I wasn't sure he had it in him. He's a cold-hearted competitor. That's what Broadway is about."

"Backstabbing?" I asked, frustrated. "You're not going to do anything about this? He tried to cheat."

"That's the industry. I would've been in Cats if not for Alyssa Buckingham. Buckingsham is more like it."

I didn't know what to say, so I was happy when other kids made it to class and it was time to start. I couldn't wait to get home and find the original signup sheet I took on Randy's first day. I needed to know if he had tried to cheat me.

As soon as Derek unlocked the front door after school, I dropped my backpack and went straight to my room. I rustled through some papers and a few books on my desk and held up the signup sheet. I checked the deadline. It was clearly marked November 12th. The one Randy gave me had been doctored to say November 14th. He tried to take me out of the competition before it even started! I pretty much already knew it, but I wanted to see the evidence to make sure.

I was furious with him, but also happy to know that I was still able to audition. He was going to be shocked. I hoped it would be enough to knock him off his game. I decided I was going to confront him in front of Sophie. I wanted her to know what he did, so maybe she could finally see what a jerk he actually was, not the character he played for her.

The next morning, the Speaker of Doom crackled above the door. "Good morning, Gophers!" Principal Buthaire said with enthusiasm, which was never a good sign. "A few housekeeping items for today. Detentions are up 22%, in part due to my keen detection skills of those students who continue to flaunt their defiance of my rules." Nearly my whole Advisory class groaned. We had heard it so many times before. "Unfortunately, grades are down. Recent report cards suggest a significant deterioration in student achievement. There is only one solution."

"Fewer detentions?" I suggested to chuckles.

Principal Buthaire continued, "MORE Detentions!"

Whines erupted from every classroom throughout the school. It was getting ridiculous. I thought the school might riot.

"Teachers will be submitting weekly progress reports to my office-"

"The Butt Crack," I said in my best Principal Buthaire voice. The kids around me laughed.

"And those receiving grades of C or below will get automatic detention. That is all," Principal Buthaire said with joy.

It didn't really bother me, because that day was going to be special. Randy was going to be exposed as a villain and everyone would shun him.

In order to expose Randy, I decided to change tactics. Instead of showing up early to make sure he and Sophie didn't talk, I walked in right at the bell, knowing that the whole class would already be there. The class was full and quiet. Perfect. I smiled and then forced my face into a frown. "Really, Randy?" I said, trying to bait him.

He looked at me without expression.

"Afraid I might beat you in the audition, so you had to cheat?" I said loud enough for the class next door to hear.

I heard a few gasps and saw a few pairs of bulging eyes. Randy didn't respond. He turned his back on me and looked at Mr. Gifford, who was watching me.

I stepped forward. "Did you hear me, cheater? Where are your snappy comebacks?"

Ditzy Dayna stepped toward me and said, "He's resting

his vocal cords. He shouldn't waste his talent responding to such childishness."

"Childishness? Would you be okay if he tried to cheat you out of something?" I asked, my voice shaking. I wasn't faking anger anymore. I was furious.

Sophie grabbed my hand and pulled me toward my seat. She whispered, "It's fine. Don't worry about it."

Mr. Gifford said, "Okay, that's enough. Please, everyone take your seats. Funny enough, we're going to talk about combustion, so thank you, Austin, for your fiery entrance!"

I looked at Sophie, my mouth open. "It's fine? Don't worry about it? He cheated. And I'm going to crush him in the auditions."

Sophie looked at me with a sympathetic face. It only made me angrier. Let the combustion begin.

9

I prepped and crammed as much as I could during the next day and a half. My voice was getting sore. I wished I had more time, but I felt okay about it.

The way the auditions worked was that you could try out for any part you wanted, but Mrs. Funderbunk reserved the right to give out the roles as she saw fit. If you weren't going for the two leads or other important parts, it would be more likely that you got the part you wanted.

My audition was scheduled for 2:35. I was first up. Great. The good news was that I was going to be done before anyone probably got there. After the bell rang, I rushed to my locker, filled my backpack, and headed toward the theatre. I entered the empty backstage area, placed my backpack under one of the makeup tables, and took a deep breath. I wasn't even on the stage and my heart was pounding. I closed my eyes and took long, slow breaths.

A squeaky voice behind me said, "Are you Austin?"

I opened my eyes and turned around. A young woman with light brown hair and green eyes stood in front of me. "I...umm...am." I was certain of it.

"Good. My name is Miss Honeywell. I'm the assistant director of Santukkah!" She framed it like Mrs. Funderbunk. "It's time for your audition."

I took one more deep breath and followed Miss Honeywell. We walked up to the edge of the stage, just behind the curtain. She turned to me and smiled. "Mrs. Funderbunk is waiting for you. Good luck."

"Thanks." I walked out onto the stage. The theatre was dimly lit, except for the sun-like spotlight illuminating a circle in the center of the stage. I could see Mrs. Funderbunk in the front row, but really couldn't make out much detail.

"Good afternoon," Mrs. Funderbunk greeted me. "Step into the spotlight and sing Joseph's jingle from the first act. Ready?"

My hands were shaking. My palms were sweaty. The sound of my beating heart pounded in my ears. I didn't think I could go through with it. Despite all that, I answered,

"Yes." I took a few more deep breaths. I looked over to the side of the stage, wondering if I should make a run for it. Thankfully, Miss Honeywell was there and gave me a big smile and thumbs up.

"When you're ready," Mrs. Funderbunk said forcefully, as if she was not at all willing to wait until I was ready.

Buoyed by Miss Honeywell's misplaced confidence in me, I went for it. I sang Joseph's jingle from act one with everything I had. My voice shook for the first few words, but when I hit my stride, I hit every note. I closed my eyes as I belted out the final line of the song. I was afraid to open them when I was done. I opened one eye and looked over at Mrs. Funderbunk as if somehow that would be easier.

She looked down at her iPad and scribbled something with her stylus. I stood there waiting for her to say something. Anything. Mrs. Funderbunk looked up at me. "Very impressive, Mr. Davenport. Thank you. We'll be in touch."

I nodded and headed back to Miss Honeywell, who was smiling widely. "Wow! That was awesome."

"Thanks. Do you really think so?"

"Absolutely," she squeaked.

Miss Honeywell led me back to the dressing room. A lot of kids had gathered, waiting for their audition time slots. Ben rushed over to me while Miss Honeywell called for the next auditioner.

"How'd it go?" Ben asked, shifting from foot to foot.

"Great," I said with a smile. I wasn't sure how good it actually was, but Mrs. Funderbunk seemed pleased and it felt great to be done with the audition.

"Awesome. I'm up in a few more, I think."

"Good luck," I said.

Randy walked into the dressing room. I could see him toward the back, sipping his honey tea. I thought about trying to get him off his game, but I didn't want to stoop to his level, so I decided I would watch his audition from the back of the theatre instead.

"I'm gonna go, okay?"

"Alright," Ben said, biting his nails.

"You'll be fine," I said.

"I hope so."

We weren't really supposed to watch other students audition. Mrs. Funderbunk wanted a safe environment for all the kids. It's not easy singing in front of other kids. I certainly appreciated it when I auditioned, but I wanted to stick around to see Randy audition. He probably wanted more attention anyway.

I slipped into the back of the theatre and walked up a short flight of stairs into the light and sound booth. It had the perfect view of the stage and was out of sight from Mrs. Funderbunk and Ms. Honeywell.

Randy walked out onto stage as if he owned it, chest puffed out, flipping his hair around, and basically acting like a pompous punk.

Mrs. Funderbunk said, "Good afternoon, Randy. You may begin when ready."

Randy took a deep breath and then began. He was a natural, hitting every note, working the stage, Joseph's jingle emanating from his pores. Randy fell to his knees and for a moment, I thought it was a mistake, but it wasn't. He slid across the floor, blasting the final note in all of its glory.

I waited for Mrs. Funderbunk's response. She didn't say anything for a minute. Randy waited patiently. I didn't know why she wasn't talking. Then I noticed her shoulders bouncing up and down. She was crying. I hoped it was somehow because he was so terrible, but I knew deep down that wasn't the case.

Even though Mrs. Funderbunk was crying, Randy looked disappointed, perhaps because there was no crowd there to cheer him. He walked off the stage shaking his head.

I decided to stick around for the next few auditions. Sophie, Ben, Just Charles, and Luke would all be performing. I wanted to see how they would do.

Sophie tried out for the lead character of Mary, mother of Jesus, as did Melody Vonn and Crystal Rivers. She stepped out on the stage, nervously. I wanted to call out support to her. I could see her hand shaking from across the theatre.

Mrs. Funderbunk nodded, "You're going to do lovely, Sophie. When you're ready."

Sophie nodded, a little more confident. She stepped forward toward Mrs. Funderbunk. She began to sing Mary's medley from act two. She had a sweet voice. There were a couple of notes that were a little off key, but for the most part, it was a solid audition.

Luke muddled through the Judah Maccabee rap about Hanukkah and the Festival of Lights, but at least got points for the effort. Just Charles and Luke did okay. They weren't horrible, but they were not lead material. I know this stuff. Chris Capipicola had a solid audition for the part of an angel. He had a good voice and was confident.

Wendy Grier was next. She walked out onto the stage, relaxed and confident. Without waiting for Mrs. Funderbunk to say anything, she said, "I've asked Randy to play the role opposite me. I feel it will allow me to get into character much better."

Mrs. Funderbunk shrugged. "Okay, Ms. Grier. Proceed when ready."

Randy walked back out onto the stage. Wendy looked

up into Randy's eyes, took a deep breath, and began singing Mary's medley. She wasn't a bad singer, but was dramatically over the top. Her hand gestures were so strong, Randy kept wincing, expecting to get punched or slapped on every big note. I was half hoping she would connect. Or all hoping.

She was also a tad off script, too. In the scene where Mary and Joseph meet for the first time, Wendy used her artistic license to, well, change some things. When she and Randy were supposed to walk together holding hands, she pulled him in for a kiss. As strong as Randy was, he struggled like a rodent caught in the vice-lock of a mighty Boa Constrictor. He was tall enough to avoid a direct kiss to the lips, but she kissed his chin and neck like a starving savage who just discovered Kobe beef.

Mrs. Funderbunk jumped out of her seat and yelled, "Cut! Cut! Cut!"

Randy squirmed free while Wendy kept trying to kiss him. I couldn't help myself. I cracked up. I covered my mouth, hoping no one would hear.

Miss Honeywell rushed out onto the stage to help while Mrs. Funderbunk called out, "That's quite enough, Wendy.

Thank you." And then to Miss Honeywell, "Benjamin Gordon is next."

I stopped laughing and sat up in my chair. Ben shuffled out of from behind the curtain like a big penguin. When he gets nervous, he tightens up like he's turning to concrete. It wasn't a good sign.

In fifth grade, he was on his way to ask Missy Peterson to the fifth-grade dance, and almost didn't make it. He lumbered across the playground like Frankenstein. By the time he got over to her, he was rock solid. He could only mumble his invitation. After that, we decided that he would only talk to girls via notes and texting.

Mrs. Funderbunk looked up at Ben and said, "Good luck, Benjamin. Begin when ready."

I wished he hadn't. I think everyone in the room was thinking the same thing, including Ben. If his voice wasn't cracking, his words came out like a jumbled mess. I don't know if he completed the whole audition song or not, because I had no idea what he was saying, but eventually he stopped. I had to crane my neck to make sure he wasn't frozen solid.

Thankfully, he was okay. As soon as he was done, his

flexibility started to return. He kicked out his legs as Mrs. Funderbunk fumbled for words. "Umm, yes. Well...there's... thank you, Benjamin."

Ben walked off the stage. I could hear him ask Ms. Honeywell, "How'd I do? That was pretty good, right?" Oh, man.

I met Sophie, Ben, Luke, and Just Charles out in the atrium after they were all done. I talked to the guys while Sophie, Melody, and Frannie Pearson rehashed their performances. I caught Randy out of the corner of my eye. My stomach dropped. I had developed an automatic response. See Randy. Want to puke.

As he passed by my group, he whispered to Ben, "Nice work."

I frowned. I wasn't sure if he was trying to needle me by complimenting Ben or if he was about to insult him.

Ben smiled and said, "Really? Coming from you, that means a lot." I threw Ben a dirty look as he continued, "I wasn't sure if it was horrible or not."

Randy laughed. "Oh, it was. I was congratulating you on the worst audition ever. I think you killed all the dogs in the neighborhood."

Ben's smile quickly turned upside down. And then Randy was gone, waving to the girls and Sophie in particular. "Gotta see my voice coach! I'm sure he can't wait to hear that I got the lead. See you later, ladies!"

Did Mrs. Funderbunk actually tell him he was getting the part or was he being his usual arrogant self? Or both? I hoped he was just playing it up for the crowd, but my stomach swirled, thinking about the possibility that he was going to win.

10

I spent the next five minutes consoling Ben. His audition had been terrible, so it was hard, to say the least. I had zero positive things to say. The only thing that could've been worse is if he somehow literally punched Mrs. Funderbunk in the face instead of doing so figuratively.

"Dude, who cares about what Randy Warblemacher thinks? The kid is such an idiot. Nobody likes him and nobody cares what he thinks."

Ben nodded. I didn't think he agreed with me, but he didn't disagree, either.

It turns out I was dead wrong. Ben and I walked outside to wait for my mother to pick us up and I wanted to puke again. Randy was on the sidewalk with five girls surrounding him, Sophie included.

As much as I probably should've sprinted straight for the bushes to fertilize it with Chicken a la Cherry Avenue, the day's lunch special, I stuck around. Sophie was enraptured in his every word, which hurt me to my core. Ben and I pretended to talk nearby in order to hear what he had to say. It's not like anybody noticed us anyway.

Randy swept his hair back like he was in a shampoo commercial or something and said, "Who is Randy Warblemacher? I don't like labels. Is it artist? Athlete? Lover?" He raised an eyebrow as he looked at Sophie, and then continued, "Or perhaps it's a scholar? Julliard's next star? It's not for me to say."

Ditzy Dayna asked, "What's Julliard?"

He scoffed at her, "It's only the most amazing performing arts school in the country."

I wanted to vomit on my bunny slippers, but they were back in my closet. I was so disgusted, I could've probably reached my closet from school and I lived two miles away. I couldn't believe how people didn't see through him. They just saw little hearts floating around everywhere.

Randy continued his display of arrogance, "Only the best of the best go there. So many celebrities have been classically trained there, I can't even count."

I shook my head in disgust. Who is Randy Warblemacher? He's certainly an idiot, but I decided to find out what else. The world needed to know that Randy Warblemacher was a bully and a fraud and I was going to figure out a way to expose him.

ONCE I GOT HOME and finished my homework, I Googled him on my iPad. I clicked on every link for at least twelve pages and I had nothing. I had three links left. I was starting to get discouraged. Then I hit the lottery of all lotteries. I clicked on a link titled, 'Baby Randy School Play.' There was an embedded video of an elementary school play. It was grainy and dark, but Randy's face was clearly noticeable. And so were the doggie ears, oversized paws, and tail. He pranced and rolled his way around the stage.

As entertaining as all that was, and it was extremely entertaining, it didn't even come close to when Randy started singing. If you actually want to call it that. It was more like howling at the moon like a wounded wolf. I laughed harder than I ever had before. I held my stomach and nearly rolled off the couch.

Derek walked in, chomping on a banana. "What's so funny?"

"Nothing," I said. I slide my iPad under the throw pillow next to me. Derek was the last person who I wanted to see the video.

"Mom!" he called out. "Austin is watching inappropriate videos on the Internet!"

"I am not!" I yelled.

"Then let me see!" Derek said, reaching for my iPad.

I moved it away from his swipe. "No!" He kept trying to grab it while I out maneuvered him. It was only a matter of time before I lost. I held the iPad with one hand stretching as far as I could while Derek climbed across me. I tickled him with my bare hand, which slowed him down as he squirmed and tried to knock my hand away with his only free hand. Unfortunately, he won the battle by sticking the slimy banana in my ear. Disgusted, I instinctively reached for it to get it away from me as he smushed it all around my face.

Derek grabbed the iPad from my hand as I defended myself and said, "Thank you!" He threw the peel in my face for good measure and took off into the bathroom, locking the door for cover.

I stood up and walked over to the kitchen. I washed and dried my face and hands. There was no use in trying to stop Derek. I had already lost that battle. I just had to make sure he didn't share it. He had a bad habit of doing that. I had other things in mind for that video.

Derek came out of the bathroom, barely able to stand, he was laughing so much. "Oh, my God. That was the funniest thing I have ever seen. Seriously, ever. I can't wait to show it to everyone. Great find, Austin."

"Give me my iPad," I said. Derek handed it over, tears streaming down his face from laughing so hard.

"You can't show anyone that. I need it for something else."

"No way, dude. That's too good. Randy deserves what's coming to him."

"I know that, but you can't. I'll give you five bucks."

"Twenty five."

"Ten," I countered.

"Twenty five."

"Fifteen," I said. We were getting closer.

"Twenty five." He was a tough negotiator, but I was confident he would compromise with me.

"Twenty." Almost there.

"Twenty five."

"Deal," I said. I was proud of my negotiating skills. We shook hands. That's how it's done, kids.

IN MUSIC CLASS, Randy and I were both there before the bell rang while Sophie hadn't yet arrived. It was the perfect time to discuss my little Labrador find.

"Excuse me, Randy. Can I have a moment of your time?" I waved him over. He looked at me, annoyed. I said, "I just wanted to say thanks. I got your gift."

"I didn't send you a gift," he scoffed.

"Oh, but you did. Well, the Internet did, Randy. Or should I call you, Mr. Woofles?" His face contorted and then went ghost white. Randy was speechless, so I continued, "Here's what we're going to do, because I'm a really nice kid and I know what it's like to be embarrassed. I'm going to forget that I ever saw that video for as long as you remember to be nice, not just to me, but to everyone you pick on."

"I really only pick on you."

"Oh, thanks so much for that."

"Is that all?" Randy asked.

I thought for a moment before I answered, "No. Sophie is my girlfriend. You are only to speak to her for educational and musical purposes. And that is going to be very sparingly. Understood?"

Randy gulped. "Yes."

I thought for a moment more. "One more thing. You are to address me as sir or Mr. Davenport. Is that understood?"

"Yes."

I looked at him with a raised eyebrow.

"Yes, sir."

Things were looking up. It was one of my top three best

days of the year. All I had to do was figure out those stupid cameras.

THE NEXT DAY, Ben and I were getting ready for our next period after gym class. I looked into the mirror, combing my hair. I whispered, "How are we going to get rid of our surveillance problem?" I looked over at Ben and watched him as he squeezed hair gel from a tube into his hand. He spread it in his fingers and reshaped his sweaty hair.

Ben shrugged. "Dunno."

And then a light bulb went off. The gel gave me an idea. We didn't have to break the cameras or hack Principal Buthaire's computer. We just had to distort the view. And hair gel would be perfect. I was pretty certain that Zorch didn't have barrels full of hair gel in his lair, so we would have to figure out how to smuggle enough past the security guards to complete the mission, but it was a start. A big one.

"Dude!" I whisper-yelled. "Let's smear hair gel on the cameras!"

"How do we get the gel up there?" Ben asked.

"Good question," I said, frowning and rubbing my chin.

"Maybe we can spray gel onto the cameras from a water pistol," Ben suggested.

"That won't work. It's too gooey. And won't get through morning security. But we've got something to build on. Let's talk after school."

It was starting off to be a great day. We were making progress on taking down Principal Buthaire's cameras and it was a fresh start with Randy.

Once science rolled around, I was downright giddy. I couldn't wait to see everyone's faces when they heard how

Randy addressed me. As I walked toward science, I saw one of the cool kids, Devan Moran, walking my way. I put up my hand for a high-five. He must not have seen me, because he didn't five me back. But still, I was pumped up.

I slid into my seat at the lab table and smiled at Sophie. "How are you on this fine afternoon?"

"Good," she said, surprised.

I nodded a hello to Gary and waved to Dayna. I didn't want to make it seem like I was singling Randy out. I called over to Randy and said, "Hey, Randy. How's it going?" Sophie looked at me like I had just farted the alphabet. Backwards.

Randy whispered, "Hello, Mr. Davenport."

I cupped my hand to my ear. "What's that? Couldn't hear you."

"Hello, Mr. Davenport," Randy said, defeated.

To say that the entire class, including Mr. Gifford, was shocked would be the understatement of the millennium.

Gary's mouth was hanging open while Ditzy Dayna scratched her head in confusion. To be fair, she was often confused.

Sophie leaned over to me and whispered, "What's going on?"

"He's just a polite young man."

"I thought you hated him."

I shrugged. "Let's just say we came to an understanding. He's perhaps a bit more misunderstood than I originally thought."

Sophie stared at me, not sure of what to say.

"It's all good," I said, grinning.

"Did you eat the Magic Meatloaf today?" Sophie said, unconvinced.

"Nope. This is all natural. No more problems between

me and Randy as long as he's nice." And he had every reason to be. "You want to meet for pizza after school? We're planning to take down Principal Buthaire's cameras again."

Sophie shrugged. "Sure. Sounds like fun."

THE TEAM MEETING at Frank's Pizza was in session. It was the usual suspects: an empty pizza tray; me; Sophie; Ben; Sammie; Luke; and Just Charles.

Ben burped the meeting into order. Sophie and Sammie shook their heads in disgust. Ben began, "If you haven't noticed, the security cameras are back up again. Detentions are through the roof. Morale is low. Rowan Downs signed up for military school. Vol...un...tarily. The school needs some heroes."

"Unfortunately, they get us instead," Just Charles quipped to laughter.

"For stealth purposes," I looked around the empty pizza shop and continued, "we will call our target, P.B." I know, we were really going to fool all those spies lurking in the dark shadows. "I thought about it all night. Sneaking into P.B.'s office again is too risky and I don't think he'll leave the system so exposed again."

Sophie said, "So, we're going to have to go guerilla warfare style like the Revolutionary war." That's just one of the many reasons I liked her.

"What do you mean?" Sammie asked.

Sophie explained, "Dr. Dinkledorf said that early in the war, the colonists would hide behind trees and in river banks to surprise the marching British troops rather than engage them face to face."

"We're going to have to pick off the cameras one by one

this time. It won't be as easy, but it's the only way to take P.B. down."

"Ben and I were thinking hair gel," I said.

"But how do we get it up on the cameras?" Sophie asked.

"And without being seen by the camera?" Just Charles added. "If my dad finds out I destroyed school property, I'm going to be shipped off to military school with Rowan."

"We're not destroying anything. Just making it dirty. We're not going anywhere we're not supposed to," I said with a smile on my face. I was getting excited to implement the plan.

"We thought about a water pistol, but the hair gel might be too thick. Plus, the whole security thing," Ben said.

"I'm sure we can smuggle them in," Sammie said.

"We'd have to water the gel down too much," I said, rubbing my chin.

"What about a ladder?" Luke asked.

"We have to be quick. We can't be running down the halls carrying giant ladders," I said. "Any other ideas?" I looked around at everyone. No lightbulbs were turning on over anyone's heads. I rested my chin in my hand and stared out across the restaurant. Justin Gant held out his phone in front of himself and Erika San Antonio to snap a selfie. And then my own lightbulb went off. "What about selfie sticks? They're small enough that we can sneak them in and out, and will extend to reach the cameras."

"Dude, that could work," Ben said.

Sophie and the rest of the crew nodded in agreement. I was happy to see that Sophie supported the idea. I wanted things to be back to normal between us. I nodded at Just Charles. He smiled and reached into his backpack. He pulled out his iPad and laid it out in front of us. It showed a blueprint of the school with red dots indicating the camera locations.

Just Charles pointed to a handful of different dots and said, "These should be our targets. We can sneak underneath them without being caught on tape. The nearest cameras shouldn't be able to capture any footage either."

"We should probably work in pairs," Ben said.

"And all hit at the same time. If we get one or two, it could tip off Principal Buthaire and push him to add additional security measures."

I looked at Just Charles and said, "Break out the schedule matrix." Never underestimate nerd power.

THE NEXT MORNING, I waited on the security line, a selfie stick wrapped up in a bandage around the back my calf. The selfie stick that I had was a little bit longer than the average one, which meant that it dug into the back of my knee when I walked. Sammie was our first line of defense. Distraction. Ben was only to join in if things went south. And I was the Han Solo of the crew, the smuggler.

Ben stood behind me while Sammie stood next to me, both of us lined up in front of different security guards. I got the one with the unibrow thicker than my head. I held my backpack out in front of me, attempting to make the process as smooth as possible. When it was my turn, I stepped forward. The selfie stick dug into my knee. I winced in pain as I placed the bag on the table in front of me. The guard stared at me, curiously. My pulse quickened. I hoped he wouldn't ask any questions.

Sammie was summoned forward. The guard pulled out Sammie's unicorn notebook. She started the distraction, talking a mile a minute. "Don't you just love unicorns? I so, so, so, so, so do. I mean, they're so magical and pretty. I just want to pet one, just once. Don't you?"

My guard looked at Sammie and furrowed his unibrow. I wondered if perhaps there was a unicorn in his unibrow. He could house a whole host of magical creatures in there. It was the Forbidden Forest of eyebrows. Or was it eyebrow?

Sammie didn't knock my guard off his game at all. He looked at me and asked, "Why'd you wince?"

We had game planned a bunch of different scenarios. I was ready. "I pulled my calf in gym class yesterday. I'm a nerd." I shrugged.

"I can see that. Did you report it to the nurse?"

"No. It didn't really start to hurt until I got home." I slid my pant leg up and showed him the bandage up to my ankle. "See?" I looked over to see that Sammie was done.

Sammie walked behind me and said, "You'd better hurry. We're going to be late."

I shrugged. The guard stared me down and then moved on to search my bag. He zipped it up with a disappointed look on his face. He handed it to me and said, "See you tomorrow."

I grabbed the bag and said, "Can't wait." I hobbled off into the school. I could see the guard watching me out of the corner of my eye. I pretended that metal wasn't forcing its way into my skin.

It all came down to sixth period. We had four teams of two. Sophie and I had to hit the camera in the stairwell leading to our science class. Sophie had a tube of the gooeyest hair gel she could find at the store while I was to supply the selfie stick. That is, if I didn't die of blood loss from the gaping wound in my calf before we were able to complete our mission. We met on the second floor. We would attempt to reach over the railing halfway down the stairs and slather the inferno-intense-hold hair gel all over Principal Buthaire's prized camera and then run into science class, which was only twenty feet from the stairwell.

We walked down the stairs until we were level with the camera. Sophie and I pretended we were just talking and about to go our separate ways while a few students ran down the stairs past us. As soon as they were gone, I pulled out the selfie stick while Sophie readied the hair gel.

"Put it on nice and thick," I said, producing the selfie stick.

"Inferno-intense hold, coming up," Sophie said, squeezing the tube. It farted.

"That wasn't me," I said.

Sophie rolled her eyes and said, "Boys."

I laughed. "Looks good."

"Do it quick. We're running out of time."

I was probably less coordinated than Sophie, but I had longer arms, so it was my job to apply the camera goo. I extended the selfie stick, grabbed onto the railing with one hand, and reached out for the camera with the stick. The camera angled down, capturing those walking through the doorway, so it made it a little difficult to line it up properly, plus the selfie was heavier than I thought, holding it with one hand. Or maybe it was all the gel.

I reached as far as I could. Any farther and I thought I might fall over the side.

"It's right there. Just slap it on," Sophie said.

Ahhh, farts! Footsteps echoed throughout the stairwell above us. It wasn't squeaking rubber sneakers, but the click-clack of adult dress shoes.

I rubbed the selfie stick on the camera, transferring a

huge gob of gel onto the lens. The mission was complete, but we were about to get caught.

Sophie whispered, "Let's go."

I pulled the selfie stick back and collapsed it as quickly as I could. I slipped it down into my jeans. The sticky phone holder was so cold, it shocked me as it connected to my side. I hoped it wouldn't solidify like Crazy Glue or anything. I turned to see who was standing behind me. I hoped it wasn't Principal Buthaire. "Ahhh, hey Dr. Dinkledork, er dorf."

"Hello, Austin." Dr. Dinkledorf nodded to Sophie. "Ms. Rodriguez, how are you?"

I cringed. I knew Dr. Dinkledorf supported my stance against Principal Butt Hair and even encouraged me to stand up against him, but I didn't know how he would handle this. He could think we broke the camera or something. He was old. Old people don't understand technology. My Gammy can't even turn on the TV without written instructions.

'Good, sir. Thank you," Sophie said, nervously.

"Out for a lovers' stroll, I see." He looked up at the camera. A gob of gel dropped to the floor.

My face reddened a little. Not because of the gel, but the comment about us being on a lovers' stroll.

"I think the bell's going to ring soon. You should hurry along."

"Yes, sir," I said, exhaling.

Dr. Dinkledorf added, "Should Principal Buthaire inquire about your whereabouts, feel free to tell him we had a meeting right about now."

I smiled. "Thank you, sir. See you later."

"Happy trails," he said. I had no idea what that meant, but I headed off to class with Sophie at my side.

After enduring a science lab with a selfie stick stuck to

my side, I rushed back to my locker and was able to transfer the selfie stick from my pants to my backpack without the camera, seeing as I used my locker to block the view. I was also grateful that I didn't tear any skin off. I closed my locker and breathed a sigh of relief. They only checked our bags on the way in, so I was in the clear.

I ran off to class and slid into my seat just before the bell rang. As soon as eighth period started, the Speaker of Doom crackled, interrupting Dr. Dinkledorf's lecture. He huffed and stared at the speaker with disgust.

The whiny Mrs. Valentine said, "Dr. Dinkledorf, please send Austin Davenport to the Principal's office."

The energy was sucked from my body. I was barely able to stand. I knew I deserved it, but I didn't know if I could take it. I got up and Zombie-walked down the hall and around the corner to Principal Butt Hair's office.

As I walked into The Butt Crack, I saw that Principal Buthaire was waiting for me. He smiled. I frowned. I felt a detention coming my way. Or a slew of them. "Follow me, Mr. Davenport."

"Looking forward to it," I whispered to myself.

I entered the office. I smiled when I saw the picture of him and his wife that *someone* had drawn on. My smile disappeared when Principal Buthaire started talking. "Security went through your locker and your backpack." Uh, oh. He continued, "We found a selfie stick."

"Okay...I had it in my locker for a while. I was going to take it home today, because you banned all non-educational items."

"A likely story." He took off his glasses and squinted at me. "Do you know anything about the cameras?"

"You're still on the cameras? I don't know anything."

Principal Buthaire look pained. "There was a recent incident."

"Oh. I didn't know they were back online."

"Don't play dumb."

"Sir, I'm so smart, it's impossible to even pretend I'm dumb."

"I doubt that very much, Mr. Davenport." There was a knock at the door. Principal Buthaire said, "You may enter."

Zorch opened the door and stepped in. He stared at me for a moment and then looked at Principal Buthaire. "Everything is clean, sir."

"Thank you, Mr. Zorch. What was the substance?"

"Hair gel, sir." I thought I saw his lip curl into a quick smile.

"Hair gel?" He paused to consider it and then continued, "Banned." Principal Buthaire cackled his evil laugh.

"Hair gel banned? Why don't you ban air, too?" It's debatable which middle schoolers need more. I'm sure he would announce to the whole school that I was the reason for the gel's banishment.

11

I couldn't wait for Friday's end-of-day bell to ring. I was exhausted. I wanted to veg out the whole weekend. It didn't work out as planned. As soon as I got home, I kicked my feet up on the couch, and the doorbell rang. I didn't hear anyone else bothering to get the door, so I stood up and groaned all the way to the door, each step more irritating and difficult than the previous one.

I reached for the door knob and missed, too whiny and animated to control my fine motor skills. I took another swipe at it and connected. I twisted the knob and pulled the door open. Can you guess who was standing before me? It was none other than Randolph N. Warblemacher, himself. Even though we had come to a little, well, rather large understanding, I still didn't want to see the kid on the weekend, let alone have him over my house.

Randy said, "Is Derek here?"

I just stared at him and frowned.

"Did you hear me?" Randy asked, frustrated.

"I did, but I found it less than acceptable," I said.

Randy huffed. "Is Derek here, *sir*?" Randy asked.

"I do believe I saw him recently," I said. "Let me check."

I turned away from the door. "Derek!"

After a minute Derek arrived and I found my way back to the couch to play video games while the jocks played basketball in the backyard. I heard a whole lot of grunting, complaining, and arguing. I probably should've watched the battle. Seeing the two most annoying people I know annoy each other instead of me probably would've been quite entertaining.

Unfortunately, I missed it all. An hour later, I found myself in the kitchen snacking on some kettle corn, one of my favorites. My mother was preparing dinner when the back door slammed, a boom echoing throughout the downstairs of the house.

"My goodness," my mother said, holding her heart.

Derek lumbered into the kitchen, sweaty and steaming from the ears. Randy was just as sweaty, but smiling from ear to ear.

"What was that all about? You nearly scared us half to death."

"Nothing," Derek said, grumpily.

I held in a smile. It didn't happen often, but that was the demeanor of Derek actually losing at something. I couldn't help myself. "What was the score?"

"I don't know," Derek said quickly.

I looked at Randy. "Do you remember?"

"21 to 17," he said, happily.

I cocked my head and raised an eyebrow as I stared at him.

His happiness quickly dissipated. "Sir," he added.

Derek and my mother looked at me, confused. I wasn't about to let them in on the little secret.

My mother handed each of them some water and then

tried to change the subject. She knew just as well as I did that when Derek didn't win, nobody did. She spoke to Randy. "So, Randy, what's your family doing for Thanksgiving?"

He shrugged. "I think just staying around here. We just moved, so my parents don't want to travel back. I'm not sure if my cousins are going to make it here," he said, seemingly disappointed.

'Oh, that's too bad," my mother said and then decided to betray the strongest bond that exists: the one between a mother and her child. "Do you want some chocolate cake?" she asked Randy. "There's one piece left."

"Sure, Mrs. Davenport. That would be nice."

"Umm, that's my cake. I was saving that," I interjected.

"Austin! That's not a very nice host," My mother said.

"He's not my guest. Derek can give him his cake."

"I don't have any," Derek said.

"Then I guess Randy doesn't get any cake."

"Nonsense," my mother said. "I'm very disappointed in you, Austin."

My mother glared at me as she made her way to the fridge. There was no way I was letting Randy Warblemacher eat my cake after I had turned the table on him. I walked slowly over to the fridge as my mom took out the cake plate.

I smiled at Randy and then grabbed the cake in my hand. I shoved as much cake into my mouth as I could. Randy stared at me with his mouth open, so I shoved the rest of the cake into his mouth.

"Austin! You're in a lot of trouble!" My mother yelled. Derek laughed while Randy wiped his face with paper towels.

I walked out licking my fingers. I'd like to think that if any of my peers were there, I would be walking out to cheers, picked up, and carried to my room on their shoulders.

I went to my fortress of solitude and FaceTimed Ben. I needed to put my frustration toward something positive-destroying Principal Buthaire and his cameras.

Ben's face popped up on my phone. "Dude, what's up?" he asked.

"Can I come over? We need to game plan."

"You have better snacks. I'll come over there. Do you still have any of that chocolate cake?"

"Don't go there," I said, my anger level rising. "Randy's here."

"What? You're friends now?" Ben yelled. I wasn't sure if I heard his voice through the phone or the window.

"No! Are you serious? He's playing basketball with my butt-chinned bro."

"Oh," Ben said, relieved. "Yeah, come over here."

I escaped to Ben's without any run-ins with Randy. And

my mother didn't give Randy our PlayStation, so that was a solid plus. We sat alone at the kitchen island, eating ants on a log- celery, peanut butter, and raisins.

"Hair gel, banned. Selfie sticks, banned," Ben said.

"What could we use to take down the cameras that we're actually allowed to have?" I said, the peanut butter sticking to the roof of my mouth.

"What can we bring into school and get away with?" Ben asked, thinking aloud.

I stared at the ants on a log on my plate. "Peanut butter. Lots of it."

"We should probably use sunflower seed butter so nobody gets killed. That would really put us in a bind."

"Yeah, you're right. Don't want to hurt any of the allergy kids. We also need a lot of jelly."

"Grape," Ben added. "How many sandwiches do we need?"

I scratched my head. "Two each? Three? But how do we apply it? Selfie sticks were banned."

"We can hide them again," Ben said, raising an eyebrow.

"Yeah, but if we're caught with them, Butt Hair will know it was us."

Ben rubbed his chin and asked, "If you were standing under a camera with a peanut butter sandwich, what would you do?"

"That is a very deep question." I thought about it for a moment. "Slingshots!"

"It'll be kind of obvious if we get caught. Even more than with a selfie stick."

"True. What about those giant pencils and a rubber band? We can assemble our own makeshift slingshot once we pass through security." I started designing the slingshot in my mind.

Ben said "Hmmm. That could work."

After a quick run to a school supply shop, we had our tools. 10 two-foot pencils and giant rubber bands. Ben placed three water bottles on top of his old tree fort. We stood ten feet away, looking up at the bottles. Ben stood to my left and held the two large pencils out in front of me. I stretched an oversized rubber band between the pencils, pulled it back and placed a rock in it. I lined it up and let go of the rubber band.

The rock soared ten feet above the bottles. "Whoa. That was way off," I said.

We tried again. I pulled back the rubber band, aimed, and let go. The rock shot straight into the ground. We didn't come close to taking out the target, but I think we killed a worm.

"How are we going to do this with sun butter?" Ben asked.

After another six unsuccessful shots, I said, "I figured out the problem."

"What's that?" Ben asked.

"Uh, we stink."

"It's too hard to get accuracy with the rubber bands," Ben said.

"We need something bigger, but that still stretches."

Ben scratched his head. "Plus, the sun butter is going to stick to whatever we use, so we've got to solve that, too."

"Yep, that's the kind of evidence that'll get us expelled."

"Back to the design room," Ben said.

THE NEXT MORNING was like the day after the world ended. It was like the zombie apocalypse. The students were soulless creatures without their hair gel. Half the kids moped around while the other walked into walls, too much hair in their faces. Well, except for Randy. Somehow, his hair was still perfect.

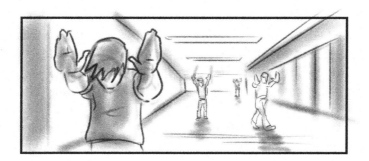

But even he wasn't happy. He stormed into science class, heading directly for me as I sat alone at my lab table messing around with some magnets. I could sense his anger. I didn't know what to do about it, but I was at least happy I could sense it.

"I thought we had a deal, Davenfart?" Randy asked, his face red with anger.

Uh, oh. "Umm, what's the problem?" I was going to let him slide on not addressing by our agreed-upon names.

"The whole school has seen the video," he said, seething.

"What video?" I asked, stalling. I knew exactly what video it was and it had my brother's name written all over it. I was so angry at Derek. Not only did he take my $25 bucks and then release the video anyway, he ruined my life again. Randy made my life miserable for no reason. Now he had one.

"You know what video," he said.

"I didn't do it. I swear."

"Who did you tell about it?"

"Nobody." It was technically the truth. Derek had taken my iPad and watched it on his own.

Sophie walked in and over to us. Other kids started to gather around, perhaps sensing a kerfuffle, as my Gammy would say.

"Let's be honest," I said, "There are a lot of people who don't like you. You're not a likeable person." Based on the look he had on his face, my line of reasoning wasn't helping. I was about to get my butt kicked in front of Sophie.

12

R andy and I stood toe to toe. I looked up at his angry face. Sophie tried to get in between us, but neither of us budged.

"What are you doing?" Sophie asked.

Randy pushed me on my shoulder. I instinctively pushed him back, a little harder than he pushed me.

"Austin! What are you doing?" Sophie asked. I ignored her.

Ricky Mulberry stepped in front of Sophie to help. He put his hands on both of our chests. Randy and I both pushed back, not willing to give up any ground to the other.

"Touch me again, Mr. Woofles, I dare you!" I am not much of an outdoorsman, but I remember my dad telling me that if we ever came across a bear, to act as crazy as possible. That was the strategy I was going with. I knocked a bunch of books off the table in a fake fury. It turned out they were mine.

It also turned out that Randy wasn't intimidated by my defensive bear tactics. Or calling him Mr. Woofles perhaps made him angrier. Thankfully, Ricky Mulberry was on the skinnier side. Randy pushed me back and knocked Ricky to the side. He tumbled toward the lab table, the momentum pushing him toward the magnets, braces first. Ricky was sucked to the table, well, like a magnet. He struggled to remove his face from the magnet, but couldn't.

Mr. Gifford walked in, unaware of what was going on. Kids scattered toward their seats. He rushed over to Ricky, who struggled to disengage his face from the magnet.

"What's going on, here?" Mr. Gifford asked, assessing the situation.

Nobody knew what to say.

"Randy, call the nurse. Tell her we have another Brace Face Magnet Case," Mr. Gifford said, calmly.

Sophie looked at me and said, "I can't believe you would do that. After the same thing happened to you."

"I didn't!" I said. "I swear!"

LATER IN THE DAY, I saw Ben sprinting down the hall toward

me. Well, it was Ben's version of sprinting. It was more like slow motion despite massive effort. His face contorted and he pumped his arms so hard, I thought he might take flight. He slid to a stop in front of me. He was so out of breath, I had no idea what he was saying to me. He spoke in word fragments between huge breaths, "Par...ts...Li...st...is...up."

"Huh? What's a partus?"

"Parts...list...is up." The poor guy looked like he was going to fall over.

My heart raced. Adrenaline surged through my body. Most of me knew I wasn't going to get the part, but a small piece of me still had hope, and all of me still wanted the lead. "Where is it?" I asked.

"Atrium."

"Let's go!" I took off running down the hall toward the atrium, Ben in slow mo behind me.

There was a crowd around the list on the wall, kids jostling to get a look, their hopes and dreams dependent on what part their name matched up with. Wendy Grier wiped tears from her eyes. She was the only one who didn't know she was not going to play the lead opposite Randy.

I jostle my way into the crowd. I stood on my tippy toes, trying to catch a glimpse of the top of the sheet, where the lead part should be listed. I couldn't see anything. The crowd in front of me dispersed in small groups. I found myself staring face to face with the list. The lead role of Joseph went to- I was distracted by Randy's scream of "Get out of my way!"

I looked to my left to see Randy coming at me full steam. My eyes widened. They were the only part of me that moved. Randy barreled into me, knocking me into Just Charles.

Just Charles let out a yelp. He was so wiry thin that he barely stopped my momentum. We tumbled to the ground together, me on top of him. I rolled to my side with a groan and looked up to see Randy with his fists in the air yelling, "I got the part! I got the part!"

I felt the air getting sucked out of my lungs. I tried to control myself, but I couldn't. I could feel a tear building up in my eye.

I stood up and walked away, not even knowing what part I got. I almost didn't care. I needed to get away from everyone. I didn't care where. I found myself wandering the halls in the east wing. I knew the exact place to go. The boys' bathroom, known as the East Wing Lounge, operated by Max Mulvihill. I pushed on the door. It opened with a squeak. As I entered, Max met me at the door.

"Oh, Davenport, it's just you."

"Yep, just me," I said, quietly.

I looked around. My eyes couldn't believe what I saw. The last time I had been in there, he had a disco ball, a pinball machine, a fridge and a massage chair. The disco ball and pinball machine were gone, replaced by a Zen water feature, an essential oils diffuser, and meditation mat.

"What the-? How did-?

Max said, "Gotta keep things fresh."

"I can see that," I said, in awe.

"Oh, and by the way, I started using that subscription model you told me about. Business is booming. You can poop here for free now. You've earned it."

I didn't know what to say. "Uh, thanks."

"You okay? Did you get the part?"

"How did you know? No, I didn't. Randy Warblemacher did," I said, angrily.

"I know everything."

"Would you mind refusing service to Randy if he ever comes in here?"

"No can do, amigo. He gets free service for advertising. He's like a celebrity endorsement."

"I thought you were different..."

I SAT on the brick wall outside the atrium, stewing in anger. Kids were filing out of the various after school programs. I was waiting for my idiot, butt-chinned brother and my mom to pick us up. I couldn't believe Derek had sent the video to his dumb friends. The butt-chinned bandit struck again. Derek stepped out of the school with some of his basketball buddies. He walked over to me and dropped his bag on the ground.

"What's wrong with you?" Derek asked.

"Let's start with you owe me $25."

"For what?" Derek's voice raised an octave.

"Uh, because I paid you not to send the video of Randy around and you did it anyway."

"I did not!"

"Yeah, right. We're the only two people who know about it and then all of a sudden, the whole school does. You've never done that before."

"I didn't do it!"

"Whatever. Don't talk to me," I said, shaking my head.

13

It was Thanksgiving morning. We had the parade on TV while everyone prepared the house and food. I didn't get much involved with the cooking. My mom and Gammy took care of most of that. I usually helped put out decorations and setting the table, but I just didn't feel like it. I lay on the couch in the den, watching all the balloons roll down the street in New York City.

My dad walked in and sat down next to me. "How's it going, bud?"

"Oh, just spectacular, thank you. So very thankful on this joyous day," I said angrily.

My dad took a deep breath. "It's okay to be upset. You went for it and it didn't work out. It happens. If you want to accomplish great things, it happens a lot. It's part of life."

"I don't care about failing. I care more about losing to that idiot. I'd rather lose to Derek."

"That bad, huh?" My dad chuckled. "You still haven't even told us what part you got."

"I got two, actually. Judah Maccabee and an angel, Gabriel. And the understudy to the lead."

"That sounds pretty awesome. Didn't you say the Judah Maccabee role was one of the top roles?"

"Yeah," I said. "I don't really care."

"Seems like you do. You're gonna do great." He patted my leg. "Buck up, dude. Mom needs help setting up the table. We have plenty to be thankful for." He stood up and walked out.

I forced myself up and moped over to the dining room. I grabbed the plates and started laying them out on the table. I stopped in my tracks. Something didn't seem right. There were too many plates and chairs. I walked into the kitchen, a huge smile on my face. We were having surprise visitors, most likely my cousins and aunt. I was pumped.

My mother was making a salad while Gammy was prepping the turkey.

"Not only have I figured out that you have a secret, I figured out what it is."

My mother looked up at me with a smile on her face. "Oh, really?"

"Nick, Tara, and Aunt Judy are coming for Thanksgiving!" I yelled at the top of my lungs.

My mom's smile went away. "No, I'm sorry, honey. They're not coming this year. We are having guests, though, but it's one of Derek's friends and his parents."

"Oh, man. I was hoping it was the Newmans." My shoulders slumped. "Who's coming then?"

"The Warblemachers. Randy and his parents." My mom said it like she was not delivering the news that the Apocalypse had begun and that the world was going to end by nightfall.

I was so confused, I didn't know how to respond. Actually, I don't think I could respond. My brain might've shut down from shock.

Derek walked in and said, "What did you say? Who's coming?"

"Your friend, Randy," mom said.

"He's not my friend! He's my competition. And Austin hates him, too! It's the one thing we agree on." He was right. I was glad my brother at least thought about me that time.

I finally found some words. "You just ruined my life and Thanksgiving forever. I'm not having Thanksgiving with that kid. I'm going to Aunt Judy's."

My Gammy chimed in, "Don't you think you're over-reacting?"

"You haven't met Randy. But enjoy dinner with him. Can I take the car or are you gonna make me ride my bike a hundred miles?"

My mother glared at me and said firmly, "You will not ruin our Thanksgiving. You will eat dinner with the family and be a good host. Not like the last time he was here."

"I can't ruin Thanksgiving. You already did." I walked out of the room, headed into my bedroom, and slammed the door behind me.

"I can't win!" I screamed. Randy had turned my whole life into gym class. My face had become the dodgeball magnet, getting pummeled over and over again. The only thing that could be worse than having Randy over for Thanksgiving was having Principal Buthaire right there with us.

IT WAS WORSE than I thought. His whole family stunk like a wet fart without actually smelling. It was more their person-alities. His mother got the ball rolling immediately as she walked in the door, her big curly hair barely making it through.

My mother tried to give her a kiss on the cheek, but Mrs. Warblemacher moved away, opting for a Hollywood air kiss.

Mom said, "I'm so glad you accepted our invitation."

Mrs. Warblemacher said, "I'm just thankful that my Randall could overcome the hurt, be the bigger man, and still want to come here." She looked at me, disapprovingly.

My mother looked uncomfortable and partially confused. "Yes, we're thankful to have you join us."

I got stuck hanging out with Randy, because Derek, as always, wasn't ready in time. We sat on the couch in the den. There was no way I was allowing him in my room.

"Have you started to prepare for your role?" Randy asked.

"A little. I have a lot more to work on," I said.

"I wouldn't worry too much about it. I'll carry the show. Nobody is going to care what you do."

"I have a very important role. It might not be the lead, but-"

"Davenport, you need to understand the hierarchy in the entertainment biz. There are leads. And there's everyone else. And you're everyone else. You're not cool enough to handle the spotlight."

I was so angry. The only response I could come up with was, "I'm cool enough. Ice cool." Whatever that meant.

Dinner was just as insulting. Before we started to eat, we had our annual tradition. We went around the table stating what we were grateful for. My father started us off with his usual, "I'm grateful for my family."

Mom said, "Another year of health and our kids' happiness. And very thankful for our guests, that they would choose to spend their holiday with us."

It was my turn. Normally, I didn't mind, but with Randy there, who knew what trouble I was opening myself up to? I usually prepared some thoughts beforehand. This time, I had been so angry, I hadn't thought about it. "I, ummm, am thankful for my family, and Sophie, and uhh, yeah, that's it."

I heard Randy's mother whisper to Randy, "Isn't Sophie the name of your girlfriend? Same girl?" I stared at him and shook my head. I almost threw a drumstick at him. I would've if I had even a 2% chance of actually hitting him.

Derek's list was really heartfelt. "I'm thankful for football and Play Station."

Randy smiled and said, "I'm so thankful to make new friends and for my parents' love and support. And to you, Mrs. Davenport, for inviting us here." He was quite the actor, I'll give him that.

Mrs. Warblemacher said, "Oh, isn't that so sweet. And after everything you've had to endure." I almost lost my marbles, but before I could even respond, she cleared her throat and said, "I'm so grateful that my baby boy won the lead in the school musical. I mean, we knew he would. He's just so talented. And Randy said there was no competition."

I rocked back and forth in my chair, fighting the urge to

scream all of Randy's shortcomings to the entire table. I could feel my face reddening. I glared at my mother. She didn't look at me, so I got up and walked out, as Randy's father started spewing out more nonsense.

I didn't leave my room for the rest of the night, which meant that I skipped dessert, a small price to pay to avoid being insulted by the Warblemachers.

Once I had calmed down, I called Sophie. She had just gotten home from her cousin's house. I lay on my bed, chatting with her.

"How was your Thanksgiving?" Sophie asked.

"Randy was there, so I'm sure you can figure out how I felt about it."

"Wait What? You hate him."

"More than ever," I said. "My mom thought it would be nice since they're new. It wasn't."

"That's...unexpected."

"You've got that right. I have a weird question," I said, tentatively.

"What else is new?" Sophie asked, laughing.

"Randy told his mom that he was your boyfriend. Or really, that you were his girlfriend. Any idea why he would say that?"

"No," she said, surprised. I exhaled. "But are you sure he said that? Maybe you misunderstood."

"Maybe," I said, not wanting to argue about it. I took a deep breath, exhaling the frustration that ignited every time someone defended Randy.

DURING THE SHORT SCHOOL BREAK, I decided I needed to shake things up. I was tired of Randy and the pedestal everyone put him on. So I got a new haircut, a faux hawk. I felt tougher. I felt cooler. I was ready for war with Warblemacher.

I hopped off the bus on the first day back, strutting my stuff. I got a few surprised looks and a few high-fives. I even got a "Sweet 'do, man!" from Damon Moore, a popular eighth grader.

I walked into school like I was floating in the clouds. That is until I saw Sophie.

Sophie walked up to me and said, "What did you do to your hair?"

"What?" I asked nervously. "Is it falling down?"

"No. It's standing straight up."

I traced the shape of the faux hawk with my hands. It was perfect. "That's how it's supposed to be." We had bucked the system of no hair gel by using hair wax, which was like glue, but not goopy.

"Oh," she said, surprised.

"You don't like it?" I asked, confused. "Would it be better if it were red? I was gonna dye it, too."

"It's fine. It's just not you."

My confidence morphed into anger. "So, I'm a nerd, so I need a nerd cut? I didn't notice that picture choice on the barbershop wall."

"That's not what I meant."

"Then what?" I asked, frustrated.

"I can't explain it," Sophie said.

"I can't do anything right," I muttered to myself. "See you in music," I said as I walked away.

REHEARSALS AFTER SCHOOL WERE A NIGHTMARE. Mrs. Funderbunk wanted everything perfect for her big run at Broadway and Randy was downright insufferable. What else is new, right?

There was a scene where Judas Maccabbee and Joseph sing somewhat of a duet. After I finished what I thought was a good first run of the song, the junior annoying assistant director, Randy, was not as impressed.

"Davenfart," Randy interrupted. I rolled my eyes before he even said a word. "You need to hold the note longer."

"Are you the director? I mean, in addition to being the obnoxious star? I'd quit if I didn't know it would make you so happy."

Mrs. Funderbunk chimed in, "I agree with Randy. I think holding the note makes it a little more dramatic. Let's take it again from the top."

I wished we were part of the movie, High School Musical, so Randy would be leaving shortly for basketball practice. But of course, I didn't have that kind of luck.

"See?" Randy said with a smirk.

"Whatever, this isn't Shakespeare's Macbeth."

"What did you say?" Mrs. Funderbunk said, two octaves higher than normal. She jumped out of her chair and her hand was shaking.

"I said, 'This isn't Macbeth." I didn't know what the big deal was.

"One must never say that word in the theatre! It's cursed!"

"Cursed? For real?" Sophie asked.

"Don't you know anything, Davenfart?" Randy spat.

Mrs. Funderbunk paced in a circle, psyching herself up. "Okay, get a hold of yourself. Deep breath in. Deep breath out." She looked at me and continued, "You must leave the theatre, spin around three times to your left, spit, and then knock to come back in."

"Seriously?" I asked.

"If you do not, death shall be upon us. Do you want blood on your hands?"

"Are you acting?" I asked. Or crazy? I didn't know if I was on a hidden camera show. Wouldn't that be ironic, given how many unhidden cameras we had in the school?

"I have never been more serious about anything in my life. One of us will die if you don't make it right. Go. Now." Ooohkay. I couldn't believe what was happening. She looked at Ben. "Let him back in when he knocks."

Ben nodded as I walked toward the hallway.

I whispered, "Do you know what's going on right now?"

Ben shrugged. "I'm pretty sure no one does. Just do what she says, I guess."

"Adiós," I said, as I pushed the doors open.

I looked around to make sure there weren't any cameras pointing in my direction since I was going to spit on the floor. I didn't care about the detention. I was immune to them at that point. I didn't want Zorch to get mad at me. I mumbled the instructions to myself, "Spin around three times. Which way was it again? Left or right. Right, I think. Then spit and knock."

I spun around three times to my right, looked over my shoulder to make sure no one was looking and hocked a loogie onto the floor. I wiped my chin and knocked on the door. It swung open and I walked in. I'm pretty certain I saved numerous lives that day.

Ben laughed and said, "I can't believe you did that."

I shrugged and followed him down the path to the stage. I was at a loss for words.

After that debacle, we regrouped and moved on to more

of my role. Mrs. Funderbunk liked to explain the importance of each scene to us rather than just have us regurgitate lines. It did help. She sat in her seat below the stage, holding her glasses in her hand.

"Now, Austin. The importance of Judah Maccabbee in the Jewish religion cannot be understated. His leadership led to the celebration of lights, Hanukkah. You will rap a song I wrote called, 'I Gotta Maccabbee Me' and then light the Menorah. It's a key scene that leads into the grand finale, baby Jesus being born, and Santa arriving via the reindeer.

I understood what she was saying, but I feared that Santukkah! A Holiday Mashup, was going to be a mishmash of a disaster. I had practiced the rap at home a few times, so with the script in my hand, I was able to get through it without any pointers from Randy and a "Good job," from Mrs. Funderbunk.

As we were walking out, Randy had his usual group of groupies around him. I heard Pam ask, "How will you do the crying scene?"

"It's not hard. I've been practicing, too," Randy said, his annoying face, annoying me.

I laughed out loud, I guess a little too loud, because Randy turned out of his circle of admirers and stared me down. "Something funny, Davenfart?" The girls around him giggled. "You think you're better?"

"No, I just have some horrible life experiences that make me want to cry, like having to suffer through every moment spent with you. Particularly, Thanksgiving dinner."

Wendy chimed in, "Oooooh. You had dinner with him? What was it like?" she asked me.

"He's standing right there. And are you his fan club? He's as insufferable on the holidays as any other day."

Randy scoffed. "I challenge you to a crying contest."

I laughed. "Challenge accepted. After rehearsal tomorrow."

"You're goin' down, Davenfart."

"We'll see," I said, and then turned to walk away.

Ben asked, "You sure about this?"

"No, not at all," I said, "But I can't back out now." I should have.

The only thing the drama club could talk about all day was the showdown between Randy and me. He was the clear favorite. Even Ben and Sophie didn't think I could win. To be honest, I wasn't all that sure myself.

We gathered in the backstage dressing area after rehearsal. There were at least twenty kids circled around Randy and me. I had done some homework on the Internet. My strategy was to drink lots of water to juice up my tear ducts and then channel all of the horrible things that Randy and Derek had done to me, and pinch my leg as hard as I could through my jeans pocket.

Randy and I stared at each other in the middle of the circle with Kenny Schwartz off to the side. He was the judge. I looked over to Ben, Sophie, and Sammie for support. Ben looked like he was going to cry himself. I wondered if I could swap places with him like a wrestling tag-team match. My guess was no.

Kenny stepped forward, "This is going to be a clean fight. Whoever cries first, wins. In the event of a tie, the volume of tears will be the tie breaker. Intentional physical harm visible to the audience is strictly forbidden and grounds for an immediate disqualification." He looked back and forth between Randy and me. "Any questions?"

Randy and I both shook our heads.

Kenny said, "Good luck, gentlemen. May the best crier win. You may begin now."

The crowd started cheering immediately. I closed my eyes and pinched my leg as hard as I could. I visualized every beating Derek ever gave me, which took quite some time. I could feel the tears starting to work their way through the ducts. I put my other hand in my pocket and pinched that leg, too.

The crowd was growing louder. I tried my best not to worry about what Randy was doing or how close he was to crying. We were both probably getting close. I just needed to squeak out one tear as quickly as possible. I squeezed my eyes as tight as I could, reliving the time that Derek and my cousins, Eddie and Gregory, held me upside down over the railing by my feet down the stairs leading to my basement.

I felt tears welling up in my eyes. It was only a matter of seconds before they popped out and ran down my face. I was about to crush Randy. And then I felt it. I opened my eyes.

I yelled, "Done!" at the same time Randy did.

Kenny rushed between us and yelled, "Face me! We have a tie. Let's see who has more tears." He grabbed my left hand and Randy's right and studied our faces.

I looked over at Randy to see tears streaming down his face like the Niagara Falls. I sighed as Kenny raised Randy's hand up and said, "We have a winner!"

The group cheered. Randy smirked at me and then turned to celebrate with his fans.

Wendy Grier and Mara Mooney were crying, too.

Sophie looked at Randy and said, "I just felt your pain. That was amazing."

I felt like a cloud of vomit had just rained on me. Ben and Sammie came over to me, and then Sophie.

"It's okay, dude," Ben said.

"Yeah, you did awesome," Sammie said.

"It didn't feel awesome. I thought I was going to win."

"Good job," Sophie said.

"Did you feel my pain?" I asked. I walked away before she could answer.

Despite my entire body fighting me, I walked over to Randy, held out my hand, and said, "You won, fair and square. Good..." I gulped. "Good...good job," I eventually squeaked out.

Randy laughed and looked at my hand. "Please, Davenfart. Don't ever disrespect me again."

I put my hand down as some kids from the crowd laughed. Randy Warblemacher just cemented himself as my arch nemesis for life.

I KNEW I wasn't going to beat Randy at pretty much anything, so I had to focus my energy on my other nemesis, Principal Buthaire. Sammie, Ben, and I stood in Ben's backyard planning our next assault on Principal Butt Hair's cameras.

My brother was at basketball practice so our engineering squad hung at my house. Ben and Sammie were with me as we worked out the next prototype of our sunflower seed butter slingshot. We sat in Adirondack chairs surrounding a fire pit.

"I think we keep the pencils, but we have to replace the rubber bands," I said.

"Something bigger, but still stretchy," Ben added.

"Are you thinkin' what I'm thinkin'?" I asked.

"I don't know. What're you thinking?" Ben shrugged.

"I'm lost," Sammie said.

"Underwear!" I yelled, ceremoniously. I looked over at Ben and held out my hand. "Hand it over."

"No! You!"

I said, "I guess I'll steal Derek's." Sammie blushed.

I slipped in the back door, which led into the laundry room. I was back outside in thirty seconds with a pair of Derek's purple underwear.

Ben and Sammie refuse to touch it.

"It's clean!" I yelled. I took a deep breath. "I'll do it."

I walked over to them. Ben held out the pencils. I slipped the underwear on, lined up a shot and let it go. The only problem was that it didn't go. The sunflower seed butter got stuck in fold of the fabric.

"That stunk," I said.

"Try it again," Sammie said.

I pulled back Derek's underwear, fantasizing about giving him a ginormous wedgie as I did so. I let it fly. The sun butter ball failed to launch, again stuck in the fabric.

Ben scratched his head. "It's too big. There's too much material. It keeps getting stuck."

I looked at Sammie, "Sammie, we need something smaller. We need yours."

"No way!" Sammie yelled.

Ben asked, "How about your sister's?"

I nodded my head. "I'll be right back." I ran back inside. I rifled through the piles of laundry on top of the dryer. I heard footsteps. I couldn't find any of my sister's underwear. The footsteps were getting closer. I found a pair and slipped it into my pocket.

My sister walked around the corner and shrieked. "Austin, you scared me!"

"Sorry," I said. "I gotta go." I turned to walk out the door.

"What is that sticking out of your pocket?"

"Uh, Derek's underwear. I'm going to put it on the flag-pole at school."

"Oh, nice. Take a pic. I'll put it on Instagram."

"No problem."

I had dodged a close call. I headed back outside. Ben was preparing the sun butter balls. I walked up to them. Sammie looked up. "Did you get them?"

I pulled my sister's underwear out of my pocket and held them up like a prize. "They're the perfect size."

Ben rubbed his chin. "How are we gonna keep the sun butter off of them?"

"Can you freeze them?" Sammie asked.

"They won't splatter then," I said.

"My mom makes these peanut butter chocolate balls and she puts them on wax paper," Sammie said.

"That's it!" I yelled.

~

LATER THAT NIGHT, we had Just Charles and Luke over for target practice. The wax paper and sun butter combo worked perfectly. The wax paper protected the underwear and would even make it harder to see through. We practiced and practiced until we could knock over water bottle after water bottle on top of my deck railing with absolute precision.

The next morning, we waited on the security line, my backpack on my shoulder. I had two oversized pencils, and a paper bag lunch with three SB&J sandwiches. I got Unibrow again. He smirked when I stepped up to the table and dropped my bag in front of him. He unzipped the backpack without taking his eyes off me.

Unibrow searched the backpack. His unibrow furrowed as he reached into the backpack and pulled out the two pencils. They had barely fit into the backpack, so I wasn't surprised that he wanted to inspect them.

He grunted as he looked at me. "What the heck are these?"

"Pencils," I said, simply.

"Why so big?"

"I take a lot of notes. Plus, it's a great back scratcher."

Unibrow weighed my answer and seemed to buy it. He stuffed the pencils back in the bag and said, "Until tomorrow."

"Can't wait. It's the highlight of my day." I smiled and grabbed my backpack.

I looked back over my shoulder to see Just Charles make

his way past one of the other guards with a smile. We were in. We just had to execute.

It was time. I was nervous. Ben and I walked down the hallway. We had two targets. Hit the main hallway camera from behind the dogwood tree in the atrium and the one inside the cafeteria. We hit the cafeteria first. It was too early for anyone to be in there. Lunch didn't start until third period. I pushed the door open slowly, peeking inside. It was empty. The camera rotated toward us. I pulled the door shut and counted to five. I looked again. The camera was facing away from us.

I pulled Leighton's underwear from my pocket while Ben slid to his knees in front of me, and held the pencils up above his head. I slipped the underwear onto the pencils and pulled out a small Tupperware from my other pocket. I popped it open and pulled out a sun butter ball wrapped in wax paper. The camera reached the far corner of the cafeteria and started rotating back toward us. We had four seconds. I pulled back the underwear and loaded it. I lined it up as quickly as I could. The camera had reached the halfway point. Two seconds. I let it fly. The sun butter ball soared through the air like a Hail Mary pass at the buzzer on Super Bowl Sunday.

We turned and ran out of the cafeteria before knowing if our attack landed. Had we stayed and missed, we would be on camera for Principal Buthaire to use to expel us. We closed the door behind us and put away our weapons. I counted to six and peeked through the door again. The gooey sun butter splattered on the lens of the camera, the wax paper dangling from it. I hoped my fingerprint wasn't on the wax paper. I wasn't sure if Principal Butt Hair was that sophisticated yet, although he did ask Zorch for a fingerprint kit after we took down the cameras the last time around.

Ben and I high-fived and made our way to the atrium as quickly as we could. The atrium was thinning out as we entered, most kids on their way to class. We did our routine again. Ben squatted down behind the dogwood, which provided cover for our attack. Ben stood this time and held the pencils out to the side while I set up the slingshot. I loaded my sister's underwear with sun butter and lined it up.

"Fire in the hole," I whispered, and let it fly.

The sun butter ball soared over Mrs. Melendez's head, an eighth-grade math teacher. She didn't even notice. The sun butter hit its target with precision. Ben and I high-fived again. I looked over to my right and almost tossed my cookies. They would've been sun butter, of course.

Principal Buthaire stood ten feet away from us, handing out a detention slip to Penny Meyers. Ben's eyes popped open. I grabbed the underwear off the pencils, while Ben tucked the pencils down his pant leg. I stopped in my tracks as Principal Butt Hair turned around.

Ben ducked behind the dogwood, leaving me, my sister's underwear, and Principal Buthaire alone for a nice little chat.

Principal Buthaire smiled and nodded to the underwear. "What's that in your hand, Mr. Davenport?"

"My...gym shorts."

"They don't look like gym shorts."

"No. No. They don't. I thought they were, but I must've packed the wrong thing."

"Give me those," Principal Buthaire said. He walked over to me and swiped my sister's underwear from me. "What do you have to say about this?" He held up the underwear in front of him.

I shrugged. "I'm not sure they're your style, sir."

Principal Buthaire was not amused. "Mr. Davenport, breaking into and stealing from the girl's locker room is a serious offense."

"I did not break into the locker room or steal those. I think they're my sister's. My mother must have mixed them into my gym clothes."

Principal Buthaire crumpled up the underwear and stuffed it into his front suit jacket pocket. "Well, we'll just have to have a little parental pow wow. Would you like that?"

"Can't wait." I grabbed the detention slip he seemed to produce from thin air and went on my way.

14

After everything that had happened recently, I wanted to reconnect with Sophie. There had been too much tension. I decided it was time for our first proper date. True, we had gone to the Halloween dance together and pizza afterward, but everybody wanted a date for the dance. Getting a date for a non-school-sanctioned event was something entirely different. Trust me, I know these things. How, you ask? I can't give away my secrets.

I was going to ask Sophie to the movies in science class, but it was too tense. Sophie was still upset with me for being rude after the crying contest. So, we barely spoke. I would rather not say anything than say something to get myself in more trouble.

The rest of the day was uneventful, unless you want to talk about my Butt Hair problem. Perhaps, I should rephrase. My problem with Butt Hair. No, not that either. My problem with Principal Buthaire.

I stood at my locker after school. As I stuffed my backpack with my textbooks and binders, I felt hot breath on my neck and smelled garlic. I turned to see Principal Buthaire staring back at me.

"How was your day, Mr. Davenport?" Principal Buthaire asked.

"Fine, sir. And you?"

"Just wonderful," he said, unconvincingly. I knew it wasn't because we took down five of his cameras.

"How was lunch?" he asked.

It was a rather odd question. "The usual." I shrugged.

"Hmm," he said. "What did you eat?"

I knew what he was getting at. Surely, he didn't think I was that stupid. "The hot lunch of the day. Sloppy Joe's. I like 'em real sloppy." Did he think I was just going to tell him I ate sun butter and jelly?

"We'll see about that. I'll be checking the records."

"Okay," I said, not concerned. I really did have the hot lunch.

"I'm looking forward to our little visit this evening," Principal Buthaire said through a wicked smile.

"Yeah, should be fun," I quipped.

Principal Buthaire's smile disappeared. "It is amazing to me how persistent your poor attitude is."

I stared at him, not sure of what to say. I was going to be late for Santukkah! rehearsals, but I didn't want to tell Principal Buthaire that on the off chance that he could somehow give me detention for it, even though school wasn't technically in session.

"One of these days, Mr. Davenport, you are going to realize that you're only hurting yourself. But we will discuss in more detail when your parents arrive." Principal Buthaire turned and walked away. I waited until he was around the corner before I took off running for the theatre. I was late for rehearsal.

When I got to the theatre, I rushed backstage, dropped my stuff, and ran out toward the stage. I navigated the clutter, sand bags and props, until I was just a few feet from the curtain. My foot got tangled in a rope that hung from the rafters and I fell forward. The force pulled the rope. Metal clanked from above and then went silent as I laid on my back, the entire cast staring at me while Randy and some of his supporters laughed. I looked up to see an industrial light plummeting toward my head.

"Look out!" Mrs. Funderbunk yelled.

I rolled to the side as the light crashed into the floor where I had just laid. "Oh, my goodness!" Miss Honeywell squeaked as she, Mrs. Funderbunk, Ben, Sophie, and Sammie all rushed toward me.

Miss Honeywell helped me up and asked, "What happened?"

My face reddened. "I just tripped on the rope."

I heard Wendy Grier whisper, "Maybe it's the curse." A few kids gasped.

Mrs. Funderbunk said, "Nonsense, children. Austin reversed the curse."

I nodded. The whole idea of the curse was ridiculous, but I was glad it took some of the attention off of me and my horrific entrance. Until Randy chimed in, "Thankfully, he's not in any of the dance numbers."

I almost challenged him to a dance contest, but I learned my lesson from the crying competition. And I'm a much better crier than I am a dancer. I just ignored him and waited for Mrs. Funderbunk to restart the rehearsal.

Right after rehearsal, it was time for our pow wow with Principal Buthaire. My parents and I sat in The Butt Crack, having squeezed three chairs where there should've only been two. My dad had come home from work early, which was a big deal. This was serious. If he believed too much of Principal Buthaire's story, I could be in a lot of trouble.

Principal Buthaire pet his mustache and smirked like he knew something we didn't. He reached into his drawer and pulled out a pair of woman's underwear.

"Have you seen these?"

My mother said, "They look like my daughter's." She stared at him, quizically.

Principal Buthaire raised an eyebrow. "Do you know for certain?"

"Well, no. I don't write her name in her underwear. She's in high school. Austin says he found them with his gym stuff and I believe him."

I wasn't telling the truth, so I felt partially guilty but also relieved that my parents believed me. It meant that I most likely avoided military school, which was my worst-case scenario in all of this. I knew there would be plenty of new opportunities to put military school back in play, but for that moment, I was safe.

"Interesting," Principal Buthaire said. "You can't confirm that he didn't break into the girls' locker room and steal them. We have strong proof that he did."

He was flat out lying. Perhaps my use of Leighton's underwear was less than honest, but I absolutely didn't break into the girls' locker room and steal them. Honest.

"What proof do you have?" My father asked, pointedly.

Principal Buthaire thought for a moment. I thought I could see a bead of sweat growing on his forehead.

"He was holding them down the hall from the girls' locker room."

"Do you have proof that he was in the locker room or that there was a break in? Any girls report missing underwear?" My mother ripped into Principal Buthaire. It was nice seeing him squirm. I covered my mouth to hide my smile.

My dad added, "Unless you have proof that my son was in the girl's locker room, this meeting is over. Do you?"

Principal Buthaire squirmed in his chair. "Well, no. You see, the cameras were hit with peanut butter."

"Well, there you have it. Thanks for wasting our time on this. I left work early. I'll be letting the superintendent know about how you're running things here."

My father stood up. "Oh, and by the way, you're lucky that we don't sue the school for the light that fell and almost killed my son. Keep that in mind the next time you go on one of your little vendettas against Austin. This is getting ridiculous," my father said. If there was a crowd watching, they would've cheered. I almost did anyway.

I stood up, kept my head down, and followed my dad out of The Buttt Crack. It was not the time to gloat. I could see Principal Buthaire seething in his chair. He was almost as mad as when his plan to down the Halloween dance was thwarted by the school's dynamic duo. Hint: that's Ben and me.

I DECIDED I needed to celebrate. I wanted to make another attempt at asking Sophie to the movies. We had our date at the Halloween dance, but that was it. In my defense, I was only in the sixth grade. Before rehearsal started the next day, I walked up behind her. She was seated at a makeup table doing homework. Our rehearsal schedule was demanding, so we fit homework in whenever we could.

"Hey, there," I whispered. I could feel my mouth start to dry up.

Sophie looked up and answered, "Hey. What's up?" She was upbeat, which was a good start.

"Hi," I said, nervously.

"What's wrong?"

My heart was pounding. "Nothing. I just, umm, wanted to see if you, you know, wanted to maybe, perhaps, if you're free, attend, you know, go to, a movie, on Friday night, with Austin, me, on you know, a date." I exhaled. It wasn't my most articulate moment, but I got the words out. A lot of them.

Her face dropped. "Oh, no. I already told Randy I would rehearse lines with him. The musical is getting close. There are a few scenes he wants to work on."

I was half angry, half crushed. We didn't normally spend time together on the weekends, and if it were anyone but Randy, I probably wouldn't have cared, but the idea of her turning me down because she already had plans with him caught me by surprise like one of Derek's morning wake up calls in which the alarm is his knee to my kidney.

My mouth went dry. I couldn't speak. My face drained of all blood. Vanished into thin air.

"Austin?" Sophie's voice sounded distant, like it was funneling through a long tunnel. "Austin?"

I snapped out of my daze. "I'm here..." I didn't know what to say.

"Maybe another time?" Sophie asked.

"Yes. Maybe. Definitely." I smiled like everything was fabulous. I gave her a thumbs up and walked away.

Mrs. Funderbunk was heading toward me. "Oh, Austin. Mrs. Funderbunk was looking for you. Can you spend some time with Randy going over some lines as his understudy?"

My life was spiraling out of control without warning. "I

was going to go over the script over the weekend. I don't think I need Randy's help."

"He has a lot of interesting perspectives. How does thirty minutes sound after rehearsals?"

Terrible. "I can't I have to get home."

"Why?"

"My cat is sick."

"What's your cat's name?"

I struggled to make up an answer. Just Charles walked by. I looked at Mrs. Funderbunk and said, "Charles?"

She looked over at Just Charles and said, "Thirty minutes."

I shrugged. "Okay," I said, less than enthused.

Once rehearsal was over, the cast and crew left Randy and me to rehearse the part of Joseph. Should something happen to Randy, I was going to have to step in and take over the lead role. Knowing that was the only thing that could get me through it.

As soon as we were alone, Randy stepped toward me and said, "I'm not going to help you do anything. You can't play the lead."

"Randy, I am so sick of you. I don't really care. Just stay away from Sophie. She's *my* girlfriend." I stormed off toward the backstage curtain.

"I already told you that she's mine. Why is *your* girl-friend hanging out with me on Friday?"

I turned, about to say something, but Randy started singing.

"I win. You lose, but tell me what else is newhoohoohoo?" he sang.

I decided to embrace my hip hop side. I rapped back, "Randy Warblemacher...stinks like the socks inside my gym locker." It wasn't great, but it was the best I could do. I said, "Peace." And then walked out.

THERE's nothing like a Saturday morning orthodontist appointment. I sat in Dr. Boras' office with my mother. I played video games on my phone while Derek was getting examined to see if he needed braces. I was next. After a few minutes, we switched. It was easy enough, but I hoped I would avoid the dreaded Brace Face. I had enough stuff to deal with. I didn't need Randy or anyone else having any more reason to mess with me.

After my exam, Dr. Boras called the three of us into his office. We sat across from him in his messy wooden desk. He looked at me and said, "Sorry, buddy. You need braces."

Derek laughed. "Ha, ha! Sucka!"

"Derek!" My mother said, shocked. I wasn't. He was normally obnoxious and things usually worked out that way. Derek skates around trouble. I get slammed over the head with it.

But then Dr. Boras chimed in. "Sorry, Derek, but you need them, too. Yours are actually worse."

My mother went white. I didn't understand why.

Dr. Boras said, "There will be eighteen visits, one per month, and they should be good to go. We have a financing plan. It's $5,000 each."

"$5,000 per visit! That's ridiculous!" Derek yelled.

Dr. Boras laughed. "No, no, Derek. $5,000 each for you and Austin."

My mother was still white. I looked at her and said, "I don't need them, Mom. You don't have to spend the money on me. Get them for Derek. He should have them. You heard Dr. Boras. His are worse." I hoped I had convinced her.

My mother took a deep breath. "No, both you and your brother will get them. We have some savings. I don't want to give one and not the other." Great, the first time my parents actually cared about being fair and it had to do with getting us both braces. Awesome.

Mom asked, "How much are the recycled braces?"

"Sixty percent off."

"No, Mom," I pleaded.

Derek laughed and pointed at me.

My mother said to Derek, "Yours will be, too, funny man."

He stopped laughing immediately.

"We also offer unlimited rubber bands," Dr. Boras said. He wasn't the best salesman. "The kids break them all the time, and sometimes eat them." He said it like he was somehow helping us out. "We can get them on the schedule early next week."

Oh, joy.

What's bad about braces, you ask? Well, first look at them. Unless you get the clear ones, which I didn't. I was lucky not to get recycled metal. They're terrible. There are so many reasons. It's like a radio station in your mouth. And who listens to the radio anymore, anyway? Tightening days. Enough said. And it was fall- sweater season. Do you know how many poor kids got their mouths caught on their sweaters every fall? And you basically have to eat like a monk. Rice and soup. No candy or gum- and those are a kid's two most important food groups.

What's worse is that my brother and I basically had to relearn how to talk. For three or four days, we just grunted like cave men, which fit pretty well with the rest of how we lived. Our house was like a war zone. My brother and I were growing so quickly, eating so ferociously that rubber bands popped like machine gun fire. It was either that or we ate them. I pooped many more rubber bands than I care to discuss. But the good news was that the flaming bags of poo died down, probably because my brother was concerned about burning all that rubber. He can be a jerk, but at least he's environmentally responsible.

15

I t was our first day at rehearsals since I got my braces. I walked backstage and dropped my backpack, as usual. I nodded to Just Charles across the room and smiled at Miss Honeywell. She stopped dead in her tracks. Her smile disappeared.

Miss Honeywell spoke into her headset. Her normally mousy voice was deeper and firm. "We have a situation. Yes, a code silver. Copy that."

I frowned, attempting to figure out what the heck was going on.

She looked at me with panic in her eyes. "Come with me," she said.

I followed her while everyone stared at me. I didn't know what I did wrong. What was a code silver?

Mrs. Funderbunk turned the corner like a tiger bearing down on its prey. And apparently, I was the prey. "Open your mouth!" she yelled.

I tried to ask her why, but she didn't wait for any words to come out. She stuck her hands in my mouth and pried it open. She inspected my mouth as I struggled.

"Oh, geez. It's worse than I thought! Who gets the metal ones anymore?" She let go of me and said, "You couldn't have waited until after the musical? This is going to ruin everything."

"No, it'sth not," I said, unconvincingly. I was still getting used to the braces and had a bit of a lisp.

"How are you going to rap?"

I shrugged. "There'sth hardly any sth'sth in it."

Mrs. Funderbunk smacked her forehead in disgust. She looked at Miss Honeywell and said, "Get him some ice. Let's pray that works."

I followed Miss Honeywell as Ben rushed in, excited. "The ticket booth is open!" he said animatedly. "The line wraps around the cafeteria. It's going to be a sellout!"

Things just got real. There were going to be actual people in the audience. Friends, enemies, frienemies. I closed my eyes and tried to compose myself.

"It's all girls, too!" Ben said.

I don't know what he was so happy about. Not only was he less than good, he froze like Han Solo in Carbonite in front of big groups.

Mrs. Funderbunk gathered us to discuss the importance of the grand finale. I stood next to Ben, Randy, and Just Charles. Sophie stood with Wendy and the reindeer. Mrs. Funderbunk said, "I cannot stress enough, how we need the finale to come together tomorrow night. The critics will love it!"

I'm pretty certain there weren't going to be any critics there. It was going to be filled with parents and sixth-grade girls drooling over Randy.

Mrs. Funderbunk continued, "We're going to run the full musical today, full songs, full drama, tears streaming."

Randy looked at me and smirked. I was still angry about the crying contest.

Miss Honeywell stepped up, "Okay, everyone. Let's head backstage and get set up."

We all followed Miss Honeywell and settled in backstage. I read through my lines, even though I knew them cold. Nobody but Mrs. Funderbunk would be watching, but I was nervous. It made everything seem a lot more real. I looked up to see Randy across the dressing room. He looked up and around the room. It was kind of sketchy.

I put my head back down toward my script, but looked up at him. He was up to something. Randy looked around again. The room was busy, everyone focused on a dozen other things besides Randy. Normally, he would probably be upset about that, but I wasn't so sure this time. He reached into his backpack and pulled out a Ziploc bag. It was filled with some sort of red powder. He stuffed it into his pocket and walked toward the stage.

Mrs. Honeywell said, "Scene one cast, please step forward to me."

I wasn't in the first scene, so I stood up and wandered over to Randy's bag. He had already taken whatever it was he wanted, but I didn't know what else I might find out. I stood over Randy's backpack and looked around. I unzipped it quickly and peeked inside. There was a mirror (shocker!) and his books. There were no other Ziploc bags or anything suspicious. I peeked my face into the bag and took a big whiff of it, trying to pick up the scent. Nothing.

I stood up and looked over to see Sophie staring at me. I forgot she wasn't in the first scene.

"What are you doing?" she asked, seemingly weirded out by my smelling Randy's bag. I don't know why.

"Umm," I said. "I just wanted to see if, umm, how, umm, Randy smelled, but I was embarrassed to ask him what cologne he used."

"I don't even know how to respond to that," Sophie said.

Good. I zipped up his bag and walked toward my table. "Are you ready for this?"

Sophie took a deep breath. "I hope so."

Me? I was ready to find out what Randy was up to. I walked over to the edge of the stage and watched Randy like a hawk. He sang and danced like the star that he was. And then it was time for scene two, my entrance.

I watched Randy every moment I could between my scenes, convinced he was up to something. I flew like an angel, rapped, and sang. Randy still hadn't revealed his secret. Until, it was time for the finale.

I walked slowly across the stage to the menorah set just next to the nativity scene with Sophie and Randy, a burning candle in my hand. And then I saw it. I looked at Randy after I lit the center light of the menorah. He was looking down as he reached into his pocket, the same pocket he put the Ziploc bag in. He appeared to hold something on his fingertip as he wiped it across his eyes.

I walked over to my spot on the stage, racking my brain while the attention turned to Sophie and Randy. I nearly vomited as they sang their duet and then it all became clear. Randy ended the finale with sobs, as Sophie held baby Jesus. He used the powder to cry! Which meant he cheated in our crying competition. I was furious! I had to figure out how to get back at him for this one. He was so rude after the competition. Not to mention that Sophie 'felt his pain' and other kids laughed at me for losing. He was going down. Harder than the Halloween Dance fell. It was going to be that epic. I just didn't have any clue what to do.

WHEN I GOT HOME that night, I went straight to the kitchen and my mother's spice rack. I spun it until I saw the familiar red spice. Chili powder! I decided I was going to use it against him. Somehow, some way.

I woke up Friday morning, still not sure how I was going to get my revenge on the cheater. I took my own Ziploc bag of chili powder and tucked it into my jeans pocket, small enough to smuggle it into school. I wasn't sure if Unibrow would believe me if I told him I just wanted to spice lunch up a little. Not with how much I had brought with me. Although some of the food was pretty bland.

As soon as we got past security and Sammie was on her way to Advisory, I said, "How can I use the powder to get back at him?"

Ben thought for a minute and said, "We don't have lunch

with him, so if you want to use the chili powder, you'll have to put it in something he eats before the show."

"Hmm, that could be tough. But I'm game."

I was nervous all day. I think everyone was. The whole cast and crew were pretty quiet during the day and that pretty much continued up until we were backstage waiting for the show to start. I iced my mouth as I went over my scenes in my head.

Miss Honeywell walked into the backstage area, a pizza delivery guy following her while balancing a stack of pizza boxes. The cast's mood improved immediately. And mine in particular. Randy's slice was going to be extra spicy, if you know what I mean. The kids gathered around the pizza tables as plates were handed out.

I made sure to get toward the front of the line. I wanted to get a slice before Randy did so I could doctor his slice the way he fudged the audition form he gave me. I played with the bag of chili powder in my pocket. There were so many kids around, it would be easy to sprinkle some onto a slice without anyone seeing anything.

Mrs. Honeywell handed me a slice. I huddled with Luke, Just Charles, and Ben. I reached into my pocket, grabbed a pinch of chili powder, and scanned the room for anyone looking my way. The coast was clear. I sprinkled the powder wherever there were big pockets of sauce. I was impressed with myself. It was perfectly crafted.

"Good luck," Ben said.

"Fingers crossed," I said, as I walked over toward Randy. He wasn't on line for pizza. I hoped that wasn't a bad sign. He stood with Taylor Blair, talking.

He stared at me as I stood before him, holding the slice of pizza out for him. "I feel bad about the chocolate cake thing and just how things have been going between us. We always seem to be competing, but we're on the same team."

Randy looked at me like I was an idiot. "I don't eat pizza. Do you think I want all that oil in my pores?"

"It's just pizza, dude. One slice."

"Do you think I'm that stupid?"

"Annoying and rude, but not stupid," I said, not sure if I was helping my case or not. "I didn't do anything to the pizza. I just wanted to make things right."

"I don't believe you," Randy said.

I may have started to sweat. "I didn't do anything."

"Prove it," Randy said, simply. "Eat the slice."

"Oh, I'm kind of full. I just ate. That's why I didn't get one for myself."

"You can take two bites, can't you? Or is little baby Davenfart's tummy too full?" Randy and Taylor laughed.

Two bites wouldn't be a problem, I thought. "Okay, smart guy," I said. "Two bites." I grabbed the slice and folded it. There was only one pocket of sauce in two-bites worth of it.

"What're you waiting for?" Randy asked.

I took a bite. It wasn't bad. I took another bite quickly, a whole pocket of sauce hitting my tongue. My mouth started to burn. I hated spice. I didn't think it would be so bad. I was wrong. I looked at Randy and forced a smile. "Yummy," I said, chewing as fast as I could, food nearly coming out of my mouth.

Randy looked at me disgusted. "You sicken me, Davenfart."

"It's mutual," I said, walking away, desperately needing liquids. I hoped Randy didn't notice any smoke coming out of my ears.

I walked back over to Ben and grabbed the soda out of his hand and downed it.

"It went well, I see," Ben said.

"So good," I said with a frown. "He doesn't eat pizza and he made me try it to prove I wasn't trying to prank him."

"Like my dad taught me, you win some, you lose some," Ben said.

"When am I going to actually win some against him?" I said, annoyed.

Just Charles raised an eyebrow and said, "If he doesn't eat pizza, what's he gonna eat?"

"Do robots eat?" I asked. The boys laughed.

Mrs. Funderbunk walked by smiling. "Glad to see there aren't any nerves."

I had an interesting thought. "Mrs. Funderbunk, I'm a little worried about Randy. He doesn't eat pizza. I hope he has enough energy for the show."

She smiled and said, "Not to worry. He brought a salad with chicken. Our superstar will be well fed and energized."

"That's refreshing," I said, as she continued on.

"If he sees me hanging around the fridge or messing with his salad, I'm going to lose again. So, who wants to add a little seasoning to Randy's salad?" I whispered.

"I absolutely want to do it," Just Charles said.

"No way, dude," Ben said. "I owe him one. He said I killed all the neighborhood dogs."

Luke said, "Pick me! Pick me!"

"Quiet dude," I whispered. I looked at Ben and said, "He wasn't that wrong."

Ben stared at me. "That hurts, man. That hurts."

"I think I need a disguise," I said, remembering the Halloween dance.

"How about a reindeer costume?" Ben asked.

"Good idea," I said, searching the room.

So, I eventually 'borrowed' a reindeer costume and slinked over to the fridge. I opened it and searched for Randy's salad.

It was hidden behind a few things. I grabbed it, pulled off the top, and then opened the chili powder. I sprinkled it in (some might say dumped) and closed the top. I wiped the sweat off my face with my hand. I must have gotten a little bit of chili powder on my hand without realizing it. Without warning, I sneezed. I hoped I hadn't drawn attention to myself.

And then I heard Randy say, "Oh, God. That's disgusting. Thankfully my dinner has a cover."

"Sorry," I said in a high-pitched voice, trying to throw him off my trail. I closed the fridge and walked away, making sure I kept my back to Randy. I sprint-walked to the back exit to change. I pushed the door open and exhaled. I ditched the reindeer costume, walked around to the main entrance, and slipped back inside the backstage area. I almost knocked Sophie over as I entered.

"Hey," I said. "Good luck! I know you'll do great."

"You, too," she replied. Sophie frowned and continued, "Where were you?"

"Just getting some fresh air. Nerves, you know."

Sophie nodded. "It's normal. They'll go away. We'd better get going."

We walked back to the group together.

Miss Honeywell called out to the group, "Okay, everyone. Gather 'round!"

The musical was about to start. I stood off to the side of a small group that was set to open the musical. Randy and Sophie stood a few feet away from me. With my back to them, I listened as hard as I could.

Randy looked at Sophie and said, "I don't feel so good."

"What's the matter? Are you nervous?"

"I don't know. I don't...think so. My stomach just doesn't feel good."

"Did you eat anything?"

"A salad. But it didn't taste right."

"Did you take anything?" Sophie asked. Don't be too helpful, sweetie...

"I didn't have time."

"You'll be fine," she said, less than confident.

I was nervous. Not because I was about to sing and rap in front of the entire school, but because my prank was going to impact the show. I wanted to give Randy a little payback for cheating in the crying contest, but I didn't want to ruin the show. There was nothing I could do, but hope he didn't hurl all over Sophie. Imagine how that would go over if she found out that it was my fault.

Mrs. Funderbunk walked to the front of the group and said, "Places everyone. Have fun out there. You've worked hard. Mrs. Funderbunk is proud of you and promises never to forget you when she takes Santukkah! to Broadway."

The first group found their places. I hurried back stage to get my costume on and ice my mouth.

A few minutes later, it was time for my angel entrance. As the curtains opened, I was supposed to be hovering above the stage and the crew was supposed to lower me slowly to the ground to talk with Sophie/Mary. It did not go exactly as planned.

I stood on the ground with Luke and Vinny Camisa behind me, attempting to clip the rope to the harness. I adjusted my robe and halo.

"What's wrong?" I asked, not sure of what was going on.

Luke said hurriedly, "I can't get the clasp open. It's like frozen or something."

"Didn't you test it before?" I asked.

"Yep," Luke said, annoyed.

I looked at the curtain and nearly peed in my pants. "Hurry, dude. Hurry," I said. "The curtain's opening!" I whisper-shouted.

Vinny grunted and then exhaled. The clasp clinked closed. Luke and Vinny pulled down on the rope furiously as they disappeared behind the back curtain. I vaulted into the air with such force that I started to spin. That was not supposed to happen.

My head started to spin a little, but I wasn't too disoriented. I felt good enough to notice a fairly large breeze coming from underneath the robe, particularly toward the back of it.

And then I heard words that you never want to hear when you are the center of attention in a theatre packed with hundreds of people, most of them girls your age. Luke whispered, "Dude, your underwear's showing."

My pulse exploded. I reached behind me and felt my underwear. Gulp. I looked out toward the crowd as I spun, the spotlight blasting my eyes. I tried to adjust my costume to cover my butt, but (that's kinda funny) it was stuck in the harness. I was spinning around toward the back of the stage. I pulled as hard as I could, but the costume wouldn't budge.

I dropped my head as laughter erupted throughout the theatre, the spotlight illuminating my Batman briefs.

I thought I was going to add to the entertainment by

spraying my half-digested dinner across the stage floor, but somehow I kept it down. I continued to spin as Luke and Vinny lowered me to the ground, the crowd continuing to laugh. The spotlight hit my face, which was redder than it had ever been.

I landed, took a deep breath, and remembered Mrs. Funderbunk's first rule: The show must go on. I walked forward toward Sophie who was lying down on a straw bed. I promptly slipped on the straw and fell flat on my back. Kids from the crowd laughed again.

I struggled to my feet. I wanted to run off the stage, but I was literally tied to it. I continued on. Sophie sat up as I approached. I began to say my lines, "Greetings, Mary of--, Mary of--" but my mind went blank. The blood rushed from my face. I looked at Sophie who didn't have much more color than I did.

Sophie mouthed the word, "Nazareth," but I didn't know what she said. She tried again.

"Greetings, Mary of Hazardous, er, Nazareth," the words started to come back. I kept going. I don't know what I missed or didn't, but I powered through it.

From there everything seemed to go okay. My rap, 'I Gotta Maccabee Me', got a lot of applause. I was feeling a little better, most likely because the final scene was approaching. If we could get through it without any trouble, I thought I could avoid moving to another country. I was still leaving the state, but I didn't want to flee the country.

I stood at the back of the stage behind a two-dimensional mountain, holding a lit candle.

Luke looked at me nervously. "One foot in front of the other. That's all you gotta do and we go home."

"I can do that." I took a deep breath and walked out from behind the mountain, heading for the menorah at the front of the stage. My walking was top-notch. I looked over at Randy and Sophie to my left, sitting at the nativity scene, holding a baby doll. Randy's face was white as a ghost. I wasn't that bad of a walker that he had to be that scared.

As I approached the menorah, I felt my nose twitch. Oh, God. With the candle in my hand, there was not much I could do. I let out a bellowing, "Achoooo!" And then an "Ahhh, pooh!" as I dropped the candle and watched it fall in slow motion. It hit the floor and ignited some straw that had been kicked away from the straw bed and nativity scene, probably when I fell.

The crowd gasped. And then I heard a theatre-echoing, "Hwulah!" behind me. I turned toward the nativity scene to see Randy's head in the manger. Sophie stood up and jumped back with a shriek, the doll in her hands taking flight across the stage.

I didn't think. I just took off running, my hands stretched out, ready to make the big play. I was going to make Derek The Destroyer, Mr. Rookie of the Year, look like a tackling dummy with the skills I was going to flash. I could erase the underwear, the fall, the forgetfulness, and maybe even the fire when I saved baby Jesus. I took one last step and dove, my eyes locked on the plummeting doll.

I grunted as I stretched my fingers. My chest hit the stage floor. The doll crash-landed nearly a foot away from me as I continued to slide across the stage. The edge of the stage was rapidly approaching. I yelped as I slid head first off the stage and landed in a heap of searing pain and soul-sucking embarrassment.

After I realized I was still alive, I rolled onto my back to see Zorch out on the stage with a fire extinguisher, blasting the spreading flames. It looked like he had it under control, but the alarm system kicked in anyway. The crowd shrieked and scattered as cold water rained down from the sprinkler system above. I was nearly trampled by Carl Lipton's grandmother and her walker. She totally overreacted.

I got to my feet to see Randy rush from the stage, nearly knocking Mrs. Funderbunk to the ground, as he blew past her. My mouth throbbed. I wasn't sure if it was from the fall or if Carl Lipton's grandmother kicked me when I was down. Sophie glared at me from the edge of the stage. I hung my head in shame.

My mother rushed to the front of the theatre. "Austin, honey, are you okay?"

I looked at her and shook my head from side to side and said, annoyed, "Did you see any of the musical? I'm the laughing stock of the universe."

I walked off and headed backstage. In hindsight, I should've known better. I entered the room to boos, a smattering of fake applause, and a few looks of pity from my friends.

Mrs. Funderbunk paced in front of us, wiping tears away. She looked up and whimpered, "The show must go on. It's true that our lead quit, our theatre was hit by a tsunami, and Mrs. Funderbunk's reputation is just a smudge above Austin's, but we must move forward."

Wendy raised her hand and asked, "Who is the lead?"

"Austin is Randy's understudy," Mrs. Funderbunk said, holding down puke. The cast groaned. I wanted to join them.

Mrs. Funderbunk continued, "Go home. And forget tonight ever happened. Although, Mrs. Funderbunk won't ever be able to do that. Please report here at 3:00 sharp on Sunday." She looked at me. "We need to talk."

The cast and crew stood up and moped away, muttering under their breath, and shaking their heads disapprovingly at me. Ben and Just Charles waved to me. I looked all around, trying to find Sophie. I couldn't see her anywhere.

I sat with Mrs. Funderbunk and Miss Honeywell. Mrs. Funderbunk looked at me and said, "Maybe we can make this work. You have a lot of talent, Austin. Why don't you sing the Santukkah! song. Let's see how it goes."

I nodded and cleared my throat. My mouth felt swollen, but I took a deep breath and sang, "Thantukkah, Thank-tukkaaaahaaa. We took Hanukkah and Chwistmath, and masthed them together."

I stopped and looked at Mrs. Funderbunk. "Thisth isth terrible."

Mrs. Funderbunk put her head in her hands and said, "Mrs. Funderbunk is ruined."

16

I went home and crashed. I didn't want to talk to anyone. Even my brother knew enough to keep his mouth shut on the ride home. When we got home, I lay on my bed, icing my mouth. My parents tried to talk to me, but I just tuned them out. I guess it was my sister's turn.

Leighton walked into my room and sat down on my bed. "Congrats. You're the lead," she said.

"Awesome. Nobody is gonna show up."

"The second show is still sold out."

"Not without Randy."

"What's the worst that can happen?" Leighton said, shrugging.

"I can burn down the school. Would that be so bad?" I chuckled sadly.

"Can it get any worse?"

"Not really, unless people die," I said, "So yes."

"Well, let's assume that's not going to happen. So, all you have to do is go out there and give it your best shot. Maybe you can redeem yourself."

I didn't agree.

"Just leave me alone."

"Maybe tomorrow will be better. It *is* your birthday."

"Oh, fabulous. I'm sure it will be lovely," I said.

After she left, I quickly fell asleep. And then I woke up to the worst birthday present ever. I was still myself. I moped out to the den and plopped onto the couch. The house was quiet. I almost pooped in my pants when I looked up to see my dad reading his iPad on the chair across for me.

He said, "What do you want for your birthday?"

I shrugged, "A new identity. A magic wand. Time machine?" Unfortunately, my life had many moments that needed these things.

My dad laughed. "Good news. We got you all three. Seriously, though. What do you want?"

"To make things right, but that's not possible."

"If it were possible, how could you do that without a time machine?"

"I don't know," I said, defeated.

"Life is a dance, Austin," my dad said. I had no idea what he was talking about.

"Mr. Muscalini says life is dodge ball or maybe dodge ball is life. Either way, I stink at dancing and I stink at dodge ball. And life."

"Sometimes you're the star, other times the supporting cast."

"And other times, you burn down the school. How can Mrs. Funderbunk possibly think we can put on a show on Sunday...with me as the lead? She's nuts, but she's not that nuts."

"Don't exaggerate. I'm trying to have a serious conversation. Let me help you. You can do this. You can make it right."

"Okay. I don't know how, but go for it."

"Is the show better with Randy or without?"

"With," I grunted.

"Is the show better with you or Randy as the lead?"

"Randy," I whispered.

"Well, sometimes, you have to swallow your pride and do what's best for the team, no matter how bad you want it personally."

MY DAD DROVE me over to Randy's house. I stood in front of Randy's door and pressed the bell. After a moment, the door opened. Mrs. Warblemacher stood in front of me, eyeing me angrily.

"Can I thpeak to Randy, pleathe, Mithus Warblemacher? It's Authtin Davenport."

"I know who you are, Austin," she said, shortly.

She turned around and called up the stairs, "Randy, you have a visitor."

Randy's voice echoed through the hallway, "Who is it?"

"Authtin Davenport, er Austin." She turned to me and asked coldly, "How did everything go with the Fire Marshall?"

"It wath ruled an accident," I said.

"I don't want to talk to him. Tell him to go away," Randy said.

I called up to Randy, "Pleathe, juthst hear me out."

"Randy, come down," Mrs. Warblemacher said. "Your friend wants to talk to you."

The thought of Randy being my friend nearly made me puke. Of course, he wasn't, but after all that had happened, I wasn't about to correct her and tell her that her son was unlikable.

"He's not my friend," Randy said. It was the first time we ever agreed on anything.

"Randolph Newton Warblemacher, come down this instant," Mrs. Warblemacher said sternly.

"Newton?" I said with a chuckle. Mrs. Warblemacher's eyes bore into me like a laser. I turned the chuckle into a fake cough. "I, umm, lovely name," I said. I hoped she believed me.

Randy walked down the stairs slowly. He stopped halfway down and said, "What do you want? Are you going to burn down our house, too?" His bloodshot eyes stared at me.

I took a deep breath. I wasn't sure I could apologize to Randy for what happened after all he did to me. He huffed at me as I stood there. "I am thorry. I wath wrong. Come back and do the thow. You're the lead. The thow doethn't happen without you...and the thow mutht go on." I felt like an idiot. I could barely speak, plus I actually had to tell Randy he was better than me. It didn't feel good.

Randy stared at me in silence. It was awkward, so I continued, "I'm thorry about ruining the thow. And the chili powder. Although you did cheat in the crying competithion."

"I just outsmarted you. As always," Randy said with a smirk.

"Oh look who'th back. I liked you better when you were puking in the nativity thene."

"Didn't you come here to apologize?" Randy asked, annoyed.

I shrugged. "Oh, yeah. I forgot. You're an amathing talent."

Randy looked at his mother. She said, "Don't look at me. This is your decision."

Randy shrugged. "The sthow must go on," he said, mocking me.

"Thut up, Randy," I said, holding out my hand for a shake.

He shook my hand and said, "How are we going to do this?"

"Authtin Davenport alwayth hath a plan."

17

I walked into the theatre and immediately heard sobs echoing through the open space. Mrs. Funderbunk sat on the edge of the stage. She held her head in her hands. I continued walking toward her. I felt terrible. The only thing that felt okay was my mouth. I had just iced it, so my lisp would be under control for the time being.

"The curse of Macbeth ruined us. It had to be the curse!" She looked over at me. "Austin, I didn't hear you come in."

"Sorry if I startled you. I can leave if you don't want me here, but I have some news."

She ignored me. "Are you sure you did it right? Left turn to remove the curse? You spit on the floor?"

I went through the steps in my mind. "I made a right turn! I can't believe it. I cursed us." Or we just stunk. Or maybe it was just me that did.

"Are you sure?" Mrs. Funderbunk said, her voice brimming with excitement.

I nodded. "Definitely."

She jumped up. "Come with me," Mrs. Funderbunk

said. "We'll remove the curse together and put on the show tomorrow night."

I nodded and headed toward the back of the theatre behind her. I looked at her as she held the door open for me. "Right turn?"

"Not funny, Austin. Left."

I smiled. "Just kidding." I walked through the door. I turned around when I heard it click.

Mrs. Funderbunk yelled through the door, "Left turn, spit, knock!"

"Got it," I said. I turned three times, looked over my shoulder, even though it was a weekend, and spit. I stepped back up to the door and knocked.

The door opened, revealing a nervous Mrs. Funderbunk. "Left turn?"

"Yes," I said. "Now what?"

She ignored me and looked around the theatre. "Mrs. Funderbunk feels like the curse has been lifted." That made one of us. I didn't actually believe in the MacBeth curse. I just kind of felt like I was always a bit cursed.

"We need a cast. I already got Randy back."

"Randy Warblemacher?" she screamed in shock.

"How many other Randys are there?"

"Mrs. Funderbunk sees your point."

"I have to get Sophie to come back." There was probably a better chance of getting the Beatles, my parents' favorite band, back together and I was pretty sure some of them were dead.

On my way home, I called Sophie. Surprisingly, she didn't answer. I thought about going to her house, but I was sure she wouldn't answer her door, either. How could I get her to come back to the show? If Randy were to convince her, I wouldn't be able to live on the planet anymore, so I went to Sammie's house instead.

I arrived at Sammie's house and knocked on the door. Sammie answered and smiled sympathetically.

"How are you?" she asked.

"I talked Randy into coming back to the play, but I need your help with Sophie."

Sammie's eyes widened like an owl's. "Really? How?"

"We talked. He's coming back. That's all you need to know." I couldn't relive it.

"What's the deal with Sophie?"

"She won't answer her phone. She'll listen to you. We need to get her to come back."

"Can you call her? I need to gather the team. We need everyone down at the theatre to clean up. The show goes back on tomorrow."

"Okay. I'll try."

WE ASSEMBLED the cast and crew at the theatre. We had some serious work to do. Every seat was wet. Every inch of floor was soaked. The harness needed to be fixed, because I sure as heck wasn't flying in with my underwear hanging out again. We had a bunch of mops, two wet dry vacs, and a lot of pizza that my dad got from Frank's.

I stood in front of Ben and Sammie. Ben said, "You get the mop, dude."

"That's only fair," I said, taking the mop from him and started moving it from side to side across the floor.

I saw Randy speed walk over to me and grabbed the mop. He said, "No. No. No. Circles. Tight circles, Davenport." He demonstrated his obnoxious circle technique.

It didn't bother me, though. "You called me, Davenport."

"There's no time to get sentimental. Circles. Tight circles."

"I'm tearing up," I said, pretending to cry.

"Knock it off," Randy said, handing me the mop.

I continued mopping, trying the terrible circle technique. I wasn't convinced. I went back to my side to side action. I caught someone walking toward me again. "Really, Randy?" I looked up to see Zorch instead. He was shaking his head.

"I've never been more disappointed in you."

I stopped and looked at him. "You mean about the show?"

"No, I was talking about your mopping."

I shook my head. Zorch, the comedian.

18

We worked late into the night and more on Sunday morning. The only breaks I took were to ice my mouth so I didn't constantly talk like a doofus. My arms felt like they might fall off. But we did it. And it was almost show time. I walked by a group of the reindeer in the hallway, including Ben. Even they were nervous, and they got to hide their faces behind a mask and didn't even have to say anything, let alone swing in on a harness or sing.

Ben nodded to me. "Good luck."

"You, too." I continued walking toward the dressing room.

Luke rushed up to me and said, "We fixed the harness. We should be good. I think."

"You think?" I kidded. "Either way, we'll be okay. I'm wearing compression shorts."

"Angels don't wear compression shorts."

"You know this how? Angels also don't need harnesses to enter a room. If you would like to fly in on the harness in your underwear, go right ahead. I will not be doing that again."

"You're right," Luke said.

I continued on. Randy was sitting on the couch, preparing for the show, doing Mrs. Funderbunk's weird warm ups. He sang to himself, "Young Yoda ate some yellow yolks and yuccas."

I walked past Randy. He nodded to me. I said, "Break a leg."

Randy chuckled. "If you said that last night, I might have wondered whether or not you really wanted me to break my leg."

"Not today. Maybe tomorrow." I smiled, until I saw Zorch. He walked toward me, a stern look on his face. He reached into his pocket and smiled. He pulled out a battery-operated candle and handed it to me.

"I guessth I deserve that."

"Be safe. I'm sure you'll be great."

"That makes one of usth and I'm not sthure you're even telling me the truth," I said with a frown.

Zorch laughed. "I'm telling the truth."

"Thanksth. I have to go eythe my mouth tho I can talk and thing in the thow," I said.

On my way to the kitchen, I saw Sophie. She looked beautiful in her white dress. "Hey," I said. "You look...kinda gorgeousth," I said, nervously.

"Thanks," she said, less than thankful, but then chuckled. "It's kinda hard to be mad at you when you talk like that."

"It is kinda ridiculouth," I said, laughing.

Sophie's face turned serious again. "But I'm still mad." Wait, what? She walked away and over to Ditzy Dayna.

I watched her for a minute and then walked away,

shaking my head. I headed deeper and deeper into the long dressing room and over to the fridge. I looked over to see Randy checking his food on the table. He looked up at me and smirked. I shrugged with a smile. I opened the freezer and grabbed an ice pack. I needed to get rid of my mouth swelling before the show. Mrs. Funderbunk would probably die if I sang her Broadway hit as "Thantukkah!"

Miss Honeywell entered the backstage area and called out, "Everyone, gather around, please."

Mrs. Funderbunk wore a red sequined dress and super high heels that were closer to stilts than shoes. She stepped forward and said, "Mrs. Funderbunk is very proud of you all. The curse has been lifted, so Mrs. Funderbunk knows it's going to be a great show!" We all cheered. "Now, go out there and break a leg!" She looked at me firmly and continued, "Just don't break anything else."

The show was spectacular. Well, it went as well as a holiday mashup written by Mrs. Funderbunk could go, anyway. Nobody puked. Nothing went on fire. My underwear remained firmly underneath my outerwear. Neither I nor any babies, real or plastic, took flight.

We even got a standing ovation. Excitement surged through my veins. And a little relief. Or a lot. The cast stood side by side across the stage while the audience cheered us. Sophie stood next to me with Randy on her other side.

My parents were beaming. My Mom gave me a thumbs up and blew a few kisses while my dad whistled with his thumb and index finger. One day I'll learn how to do that. Even though it's kinda disgusting. Leighton was bouncing up and down, clapping. I think I even saw my brother, Derek's, hands connect once or twice.

Miss Honeywell called out from the side of the stage, "Grab hands and bow!"

I grabbed hold of Sarah Vessey's hand and reached for Sophie's to my left. She swatted my hand away. It hurt my heart more than my hand, but that kind of stung, too. I bowed while staring at Sophie. She refused to make eye contact with me.

Miss Honeywell yelled, "Randy, step forward. Take a bow!" Randy did as he was told. He didn't need to be told twice. He hopped forward smiling ear to ear and took a bow worthy of a royal prince, which I'm sure he thinks he is. He even waved like he was in a royal parade.

"Sophie, you're next!"

Sophie stepped forward, all smiles, while the crowd went wild.

Out of the corner of my eye, I saw Wendy Grier rushing toward me from behind the line of the cast and crew. My first thought was that she was going to attack Sophie. Instinctively, I stepped back and thrust out my hip, just as Miss Honeywell called out, "Austin!"

Wendy fell to the stage and skidded across the floor. I looked out at the crowd and sheepishly stepped forward. Randy was laughing while Sophie looked confused. I bowed to the crowd, taking in all of the cheers. After all I had been through to get to this point, I deserved it.

As the curtain closed, I stepped back in line and saw Wendy forcing her way in between Sophie and Randy, trying to get a piece of the spotlight with her love, Randy. Oops. I shouldn't have knocked her down. It was unlikely that Randy would fall for her, but I didn't want to keep them apart, because I'd be the happiest guy in the world if Randy wasn't interested in Sophie anymore. But I had no such luck. I was just happy that the show went so well.

Once the show was over, I ran over to my family as they saw me, and ran toward me.

"Congratulations, baby!" My mom yelled and hugged me.

Leighton stepped forward and handed me flowers. "Congrats and sorry about the flowers. I tried to tell Mom."

"We all did," my dad added.

"I didn't," Derek said. Thurprithe, thurprithe.

"I don't want flowers," I said.

My mom said, "They're for Sophie for her performance." They all laughed.

I joined in. "You got me." I looked around. "I can't sthee her anywhere."

"Go find her," my dad said. "You turned this show around. You can turn that around, too."

I nodded and headed into the crowd, searching each group of people, but couldn't find Sophie anywhere. I bumped into someone and turned around. "Sorry," I said.

Mr. Muscalini stood in front of me with a tear in his eye.

"Did you like the performance, thir?"

"No, it was terrible."

I frowned. "Ith that why you're crying?"

"No. I'm just so darn proud of you." He clapped me on the shoulder, nearly knocking me over.

"For what? Getting back up off the mat after losthing? Bringing the team back together?"

"No, that was one heck of a box out. You might have some basketball potential after all."

"Maybe, thir. Maybe." I let him have his moment, because even if he hated our performance, it was my moment and I was proud of what we accomplished. Minus the underweared angel (don't ever call me that, by the way), fire outbreak, puking, and baby dropping.

19

I could barely sleep that night. I worried that Sophie hated me. I wanted to figure out a way to make things right. If that was even possible. Ever since Randy had arrived, my relationship with her had been like a Six Flags roller coaster. Without the seat belts. And missiles and asteroids heading toward said roller coaster. I racked my brain for ways to fix things. I had nothing. I woke up feeling like I hadn't slept in days. My eyes felt like a thousand pounds each. I slid out of my bed, but my feet somehow missed the floor, and I crumpled to the ground. I rolled to my side and saw something odd under my door.

I had no energy to get up off the floor, so I rolled to the door. After two rolls, I reached out my hand for the shiny, white piece of paper, but missed. I rolled again. I stared at the paper from about an inch away. It was blank. I flipped it over to find a picture. Another piece of artwork from Derek of his favorite subject: me and my shortcomings.

It was a picture of me during the first night's performance, dangling from the harness, my underwear showing for the entire theatre to see. At first, anger started to bubble up, but the longer I stared at it, the more I liked it and the more I realized that Derek had actually helped me out big time. I know he didn't mean to help me, but it did.

I hopped up and got dressed. I worked out my Sophie plan while I threw on my sweater and jeans. I scrambled for my phone and then headed to the bathroom to brush my teeth and comb my hair.

Once I was finished, I ran back to my room, I grabbed the picture of me and ran to the foyer. I picked up an old picture of Derek playing football. I took the picture out and replaced it with mine. I wrapped the frame in striped wrapping paper and stuffed it into my backpack. For the finishing touches, I grabbed the flowers my mother had gotten me to give to Sophie the previous night.

I walked out to the kitchen. My dad sat at the kitchen table. He looked up at me from his iPad. He didn't even say anything. He stood up and grabbed his keys.

"Your car service is ready when you are, Mr. Davenport." I smiled. I was thankful I didn't have to ride my bike to Sophie's in the cold. I was also thankful my dad didn't call me, Mr. Davenfart.

I was quiet on the drive over. My dad looked back at me in the rear-view mirror. "What's going on in that big brain of yours?"

"Just writing a sthong," I said. Oh, no. My mouth was swelling again. "I can't thpeak or sthing."

"Should we make an ice stop?" My dad asked.

I thought about it for a minute. "No, the thow musth go on."

We rolled to a stop in front of Sophie's house. I saw the light on in her room. I just had to get her attention. But how? I could've knocked on the door, but with what I had planned, I needed some distance.

"Thankth, Dad."

"I'm here if you need me."

I got out of the car and stood on the sidewalk. I texted her, 'Look out your window." And waited. And waited. I called her on the phone. She didn't pick up.

I turned around and opened the car door. "What's up?" my dad asked.

"Any chanth you could teach me to throw a rock or an acorn at Sthophie's window?" I knew without my dad's help, it was not going to happen. I might not even be able to hit the mailbox and I was basically leaning on it.

"Umm, I don't think that's possible, bud." Thanks for the confidence, Dad. He continued, "Do you want me to do it for you?"

"No. I need to do this myself." And then I figured it out. I reached into my backpack and pulled out the two oversized pencils we used to take out Principal Butt Hair's cameras with sun butter. All I needed was underwear. "You don't happen to have bikini briefs on, do you?"

My dad looked at me, confused. "No, what in the heck are you planning?"

"You don't want to know." I took off my jacket and opened the door to the back seat. I put the jacket on my lap and proceeded to take off my jeans and underwear. I put my jeans back on and hopped out of the car, underwear in hand.

"Austin, are you sure about this? What are you going to do with that?"

"What I do bestht."

"Burp the alphabet?"

"Dad, really? That's what you think I do bestht?"

"I'm sorry. You and Ben are really good at that. I like when you do the duet."

"It isth pretty good, but I gotta go. I'm on a mithion." I slammed the door shut and stuffed the underwear into my jeans pocket. I jabbed the two pencils into the cold ground until they stood solidly. Then I grabbed the underwear and folded it over, making it very thin across. I stretched it across the two pencils. I searched the ground for something to sling shot up to her window. I saw a rock, but thought better of it. I grabbed a few nearby acorns and fired one.

The acorn soared through the air. It smacked into the garage door, too low to get Sophie's attention. I let another one fly, this time higher. I connected with the shutter next to her window. I held my breath, hoping Sophie would step to the window. But she didn't. I needed to make a bigger Sophie magnet. I grabbed a handful of acorns and stuffed as many as I could into the underwear slingshot and let it fly. I let out a war cry as they arced through the air, heading for the target.

I bent sideways, attempting to sway the acorns left, but they didn't budge. Still, they connected with her shutters one after the other, at least eight of them connecting. I stared up at the window waiting for some sort of sign. After a minute, I saw Sophie's head pop into the window with a frown. I didn't know sign language, so I did my best charades impression, telling her to open the window. She did.

Sophie stuck her head out of the window with a frown. "What are you doing?" she asked, annoyed.

I walked toward her window and sang out at the top of my lungs, "I'm thorry, thweet Thophie. I wath tho wrong not to twust you. But you did mith my birthday and thpend too much time with Randy."

If you haven't noticed already, I pretty much made a fool of myself. So it was like any other minute of my life. Sophie shut the window and disappeared. I wasn't sure if she was coming down to see me or not. She had flip flopped back and forth between happy and sad, I had no idea what to expect.

After a minute, the front door clicked open and Sophie walked out onto the porch.

"You are unbelievable," she said with a straight face.

"You sthill like me?" I asked, unsure.

"I always will. Nobody makes me laugh like you." Sophie smiled.

"Thumtimes I'm not trying to make you laugh."

Sophie laughed. "That's okay. I pretend that you are."

I reached into my bag and pulled out the flowers. "These are for you," I said, handing them to her.

"They're so beautiful," she said, admiring them. She leaned in and held out her arm to give me a hug. I stepped into it and hugged her.

"I'm sorry, too, if I made you feel bad."

"You did, but itsth okay."

And that's how it's done, kids. Or at least that's how a goofball like me does it. You probably don't want to try any of this at home.

And, I may have spoken too soon. Sophie looked over at the slingshot. "What is that?" It was my tighty whitey underwear.

"Umm, nothing. Just some old...t-shirt."

"It looks like underwear," Sophie said, laughing.

"It'sth definitely not underwear."

"Let me see it then?"

"Okay, ith my underwear," I said, defeated. She laughed harder. My cheeks reddened. I had to change the subject.

And then I had a great idea. "Do you want to go caroling with usth on Wenthday night? It'sth kind of a family tradition. We wear terrible sthweaters and walk around the neighborhood sthinging holiday sthongs. I love it becausthe, well, I like thinging, and becausthe Derek hates it. My parents uthed to make Derek dress up like Rudolph with a shiny, red nose. It wasth awesthome."

"People still do that?" Sophie asked.

"I think we're the latht." I smiled, sheepishly.

"That sounds fun. I'd really like that."

"Oh, and I have a prethent for you. It's not anything crazy, but I think you'll like it." I handed her the present from behind my back.

Sophie looked at it and furrowed her brow. "What is it? Is it a book? Picture frame?"

"I don't know. You'll have to open it."

"You don't know what is it?"

"I do. I jutht don't want to tell you."

Sophie unwrapped the present, revealing a silver picture frame with a photo of me inside. "Oh, my God! It's awesome." She started laughing uncontrollably. It was the picture of me dressed as an angel, dangling from the harness with my underwear hanging out.

"My brother took it for me. He'sth helpful like that."

"You couldn't have picked a better gift, even though you made me drop baby Jesus."

"Yeah, I'm thorry about that. But Randy shouldn't have cheated in the crying contestht."

"True. And the fire?" Sophie asked.

"Not my bethst work. But I made up for it, though. We made Sthantukkah history. And thomehow Mrs. Funderbunk is back to believing she's going to make it to Broadway thomeday. The world isth asth it should be."

So, Sophie joined us for caroling. We warmed up at the house for a little bit and then dressed in our warmest gear. We all waited for my mother in the foyer. She entered with a tray of mugs filled with hot chocolate. "Okay, I think we're ready," she said.

"Where are we going?" Leighton asked. "Can it be somewhere that doesn't have any high school kids?"

"Or middle school?" I added.

"Or people?" Derek asked.

"Don't worry," my mother said, simply.

"I'm worrying," Leighton said.

We continued walking through the neighborhood, singing softly to practice.

"Why don't we stop at the Mortensens? They don't have kids," Leighton said.

"I said, 'don't worry,' didn't I?" my mother responded.

'That's why they're worrying, Mom," I said. I looked around and said, "Why does this look familiar?"

"I don't know," my mother said playfully.

We walked up the dark walkway, single file and then spread out in front of the front door, my brain still trying to compute why it looked so familiar. My father rang the bell.

I looked at Sophie and said, "Why do I feel like I've been here before?"

She shrugged. My mother said, "I can't tell you. It's a surprise."

And then it clicked. "Oh, no. Mom! No."

My mom smiled and said, "I thought it would be fun to welcome the Warblemachers to the neighborhood!"

You've got to be kidding me! Randy opened the door with a frown. I shook my head as we started to sing 'Silent Night'. Randy's parents gathered in the doorway, first surprised, then happy.

When we were finished, Randy's parents clapped, while Randy looked at us and said, "That was a little too pitchy, Davenfart."

Unbelievable.

20

BOOK 3 PREVIEW CHAPTER

MIDDLE SCHOOL MAYHEM: THE SCIENCE (UN)FAIR

News flash. A new research study shows what we all already knew. No, chocolate milk does not come from brown cows. And no, kids don't really have a dessert stomach and a regular meal stomach. I'm talking about how middle school stinks, well, worse than adolescent kids stink in middle school. I mean, geez, would it kill these kids to take a test sniff every once in a while? And while we're on the subject, body spray does not equal a shower.

Some kids might like middle school because they're popular and their parents don't care if they get C's as long as they play sports, but for me, middle school was, well, different. It was my first year and I already had three nemesises. Is that a word? Nemeses? Nemesi? Whatever you call them, I had three of them, gunning for me from day one. Literally. My older brother, Derek, was one of them. He and his dumb butt chin have taunted me since the day I was born. I had the misfortune of being born eleven months after my brother, which puts me and his two butts in the same grade.

As if that wasn't bad enough, the school's most popular

kid had it out for me AND had a crush on my girlfriend. Oh, and the principal hated my guts and blamed me for just about everything that went wrong in the school. Full disclosure, it was only my fault about ten percent of the time. And he started it. But Principal Buthaire just saw the worst in me. If only he knew I was the one who coined his nickname, "Prince Butt Hair."

The next chapter in my middle school saga at Cherry Avenue Middle School began innocently enough as I entered my science class on a Monday afternoon. I was early as usual, which meant only a handful of students were there. Typically, I ended up chatting with my teacher, Mr. Gifford. I loved science and he was a pretty fun guy, although he didn't always have the best handle on his personal life.

I strolled into the lab and plopped my books on the lab table as Mr. Gifford walked over to me with a smile.

"Nice turtleneck, sir. Goes great with the sports coat," I said with a thumbs up. I wasn't much of a fashion guru, but the college professor look wasn't exactly cutting edge.

"Thanks. What do you think of the beard?" He asked. I had recommended he grow a beard a few months back.

"Looking good," I said. I was afraid to ask if he had gotten any dates. He answered my question without me asking it.

"I have a new lady friend. Two months so far," he said, pleased with himself.

"That's great. I knew the beard would work."

"Yeah, she really likes it. I met her online. Filled out a bunch of questions and so did she and it said we're a perfect match!" He thought for a moment and then continued, "Although it's not always perfect. She doesn't like science. Any advice?"

I shrugged. "I'm eleven."

"Yeah, but you and Sophie are what I aspire to be with Audrey." Sophie was my girlfriend of a few months.

This was all getting way too complicated for me. "That's great. Maybe do a science lab with her or something. Maybe she'll learn to love it."

"Like dissect a frog?" Mr. Gifford asked.

"Not sure that's a great idea."

HE RUBBED HIS BEARD. "Yeah, she likes reptiles, so cutting them up probably wouldn't work."

Mr. Gifford reached up onto a shelf and grabbed a container of fish food. "Don't tell anyone, but since you're my favorite student, I'm putting you in charge of feeding Boomer. He's not eating much. I think he's mad at me for spending so much time with Audrey. She doesn't really like him, either."

I wasn't going to question why somebody would actually dislike a fish or whether or not fish had emotions. He was the science whiz, so I just nodded. We walked over to the fish tank behind my lab table. Boomer was a pretty chill angel fish. I wasn't sure if it was white with black stripes or black with white stripes. I have the same problems with zebras.

Mr. Gifford handed me the fish food and said, "Just give him a pinch every day and a little extra on Fridays."

"Pinch his cheeks or his butt?" I asked, trying not to laugh.

Mr. Gifford cracked up. "Good one, Austin."

"Seriously, I will take good care of him."

We stared at Boomer zip around the tank as I dropped a pinch of food on top of the water.

"Isn't it so peaceful? Did you ever just want to be a fish?" Mr. Gifford asked.

"Not really." Things were getting weird fast.

Mr. Gifford didn't seem to hear me. "Just leave all your troubles behind and hit the open sea?"

"It's dangerous out there, sir. Didn't you see Nemo?"

"Yeah, but the E.A.C. is totally rad." He gave me the surfer's hang loose sign and smiled. The bell rang, interrupting us.

MR. GIFFORD TURNED AROUND and said, "Okay, everyone. Settle down and listen up. I hope everyone had a great weekend. This is the start of my favorite time of year. I have good news."

Jake Gillespie called out, "Class is canceled?" Everyone cheered.

"No, no," Mr. Gifford said.

"Principal Buthaire quit?" Jake asked. Everyone cheered louder.

"No. One month from today, we will have the 44th annual Cherry Avenue Middle School Science Fair!"

I yelled out, "Yes!" and cheered wildly. I was actually pretty stoked about it. I loved science and knew I could win the whole thing. I looked around to see that I was the only one who seemingly felt that way, or at least was willing to show it to his peers. Everyone stared at me, even Sophie. I could feel my face flush red faster than a turbo toilet.

Mr. Gifford broke through the awkwardness. "Well that's the spirit, Austin!" and then continued, "Here's how it works."

I put my head down and started taking notes, ignoring the chuckles from Randy and others.

Mr. Gifford laid out the rules. "You can work alone or with one other partner. You cannot spend more than $200. I recommend a timeline and explanation of your project on a poster board. And you must present your project to the judges in an oral presentation."

"I'm out!" Kevin McManus said to chuckles.

My nemesis, Randy asked, "What do we get if we win?" Like he was gonna win.

"Good question, Mr. Warblemacher. You get Gopher pride," he said. Like anybody cared about that.

The class erupted into boos.

Mr. Gifford tried to salvage the situation, "And a really, nice medal, made of plastic..." His voice trailed off. Mr. Gifford shrugged to more boos, knowing his answer stunk. "Sorry. Budget cuts. But," he held up his index finger. "You also get bragging rights."

Great. Let's allow the winners to taunt the losers. Sounds like gym class for nerds. I didn't need bragging rights. I just liked building stuff, so I was in no matter what.

As if the science fair excitement wasn't enough (actually, for most, it wasn't), another bombshell dropped just after the eighth period bell. I stood at my locker, stuffing my backpack with notebooks and textbooks. Just Charles (don't dare call him Charlie or Chuck) walked up and spun the dial on his lock.

"Dude, I can't believe you didn't tell any of us."

I had no idea what he was talking about. "Umm, about what?"

"The website."

"I don't know anything about any website," I said. I threw up my hands. "Honest." I was always getting blamed for stuff. Forgive me if I was a little defensive.

Justin Allen walked by and whispered, "Nice work, Austin. You really got Butt Hair."

I turned around confused. I checked my pants, wondering if somehow my butt had actually grown hair and was out for everyone to see. Luckily, my jeans were still firmly attached to my waist and there was no sign of butt hair.

Just Charles opened his locker and then stared at me. "You really don't know? You didn't hear anything about Principal Buthaire's website?

My shoulders dropped. I wished it was my butt hair. I didn't need another confrontation with Principal Buthaire. "What's on the website?"

"It lists so many different things. But basically, just bashing Prince Butt Hair at every turn, many of your battles."

"Really?" This was not good. Like, not at all.

"Dude, everyone thinks you did it."

Oh, farts. "What? Oh, man. If everyone thinks I did it, then Butt Hair thinks I did it. He's gonna be on me like a smug look on Randy Warblemacher's face." Which was basically permanently.

"Dang, bro. Here he comes." Just Charles pointed down the hallway behind me.

I turned around to see Principal Buthaire heading down the hall, a man on a mission, checking everyone's faces in the small clusters of kids. In middle school, kids walk around like pack animals to avoid being easy prey for the mean kids. Herding is a survival mechanism. Whether you're a zebra or a tween, it works. Well, it works when your herd doesn't leave you in the dust.

I turned back to Just Charles, my herd, for some support, but he was gone. Double farts. That's why he wasn't my best friend. Ben would still be there. He'd be frozen stiff, but still, I'd feel better knowing he was behind me, thinking positive thoughts or whatever went on inside his head when he was frozen.

I slammed my locker quickly, knowing full well that I didn't have all my books. With my grades, I could afford to miss a homework or two. I slipped my backpack onto my shoulder and turned away from Principal Buthaire. I started to run, but was jerked backward. At first, I thought that Butt Hair had somehow caught up to me and grabbed onto my backpack with Hulk-like strength or maybe even lassoed me with his braided butt hair. I turned quickly and saw Principal Buthaire continuing to make his way toward me and that my shoulder strap was caught in the locker.

Principal Buthaire's voice echoed throughout the hallway. "Mr. Benson, you're late."

"But sir, school's over," Thomas Benson said in a high-pitched voice. At least Principal Buthaire was consistent in his unfairness.

"Well, I'm sure you're late for something. Your mother is probably waiting for you. She is, isn't she?"

"Yes, sir," Thomas said, defeated.

Instead of opening my locker back up, I grappled with the strap, struggling to pull it from behind the door. I forced it loose with a grunt and stumbled, nearly falling over. I turned on my heels with Principal Buthaire only one herd of kids behind me. I raced around a few kids, who were also scattering at the approaching Principal of Darkness.

"Mr. Davenport!" I heard Principal Buthaire call out. "I need a word with you!"

We would be having no words. Not even one. Not until I figured out more about this website and why I was going to get blamed for it. I continued down the hall until I saw

Randy heading my way, a pack of his brute squad at his side. I stopped dead in my tracks. No matter which way I went, I would have a run in with one of my nemeses (I think I got it right this time). I looked to my left and saw an open classroom door. I scooted in quickly, not sure if Prince Butt Hair saw me enter or not.

I found myself face to face with Amanda Gluskin. Like face to face. So close that she looked like a Cyclops. You know what I'm talking about. I felt her tuna breath on my face and then up my unprotected nose. It was less than exciting. I nearly hurled.

"Austin," she whispered. "I didn't know you were so into me."

I backed up, Amanda's one eye becoming two again. I didn't know what to say. She wasn't the kind of girl you wanted to make angry. Her emotional outbursts were legendary. She once wrestled Mr. Muscalini over a confiscated note and won, forcing him into submission through the Camel Clutch. She was no joke. And also not great at reading situations. I was not at all into her.

"I just got turned around. I'm sorry to run into you like that." I wanted to run away. Fast. But I heard Principal Buthaire talking outside the classroom, so I was stuck for a while.

"I thought you had a girlfriend."

"I do. How's, umm, your dating life going?" I regretted it immediately. She didn't have a dating life. Nobody had the guts to date her. Or the wrestling technique.

"It's better than ever," she said, raising an eyebrow.

"Oh, really?" I asked, surprised. "How so?"

"You're here."

Amanda stepped forward, licking her lips like I was a giant cheeseburger deluxe from Burger Boys.

"Well, it's been great, but I gotta go." I'd rather get accosted by Principal Buthaire than lovingly ingested by Amanda Gluskin. I turned quickly and sprinted from the room.

"Text me!" Amanda yelled after me.

I turned left at the corner and made another quick right turn, likely out of sight and reach of Principal Buthaire. I avoided a skirmish, but the war was still going, and the next battle was probably coming soon.

I still had to make it to Derek's locker and get to the bus. On days when Derek and I didn't stay after, I had to help him with his backpack. I know, not fair. The doofus broke his foot during a basketball game. We actually bonded over it a little because it was all Randy's fault. I know, what else is new? Randy Warblemacher: destroyer of all that is decent. Well, that might be a stretch to say my brother was decent, but at that particular moment in time, Randy was my biggest foe, so the enemy of my enemy was my friend. Sort of.

Derek leaned forward on his crutches, his casted foot in the air behind him. "What took you so long?" he asked, annoyed.

There was no way I was going to mention Amanda Gluskin. I would never live that one down. And who knows what lengths my brother would go trying to set us up and ruin my life?

"I had to implement evasive maneuvers. Buthaire was on my trail. Sorry, Derek."

"You can call me Mr. Davenport," he said like an idiot. Nothing new there.

"I'm not your butler," I said, annoyed. "Besides, there are a lot of other things I'd rather call you than that."

Derek picked up and threw his backpack a few feet in front of me. "Let's go."

I shook my head. Derek swung through the hallway on his crutches. I took a few steps like a field goal kicker, took aim at the back of Derek's head, and surged forward.

"Davenport for the game winner!"

My foot connected with Derek's bag and almost shattered. "Owww!" I yelled. Apparently, kicking a bag full of textbooks was slightly different than a piece of leather filled with air. My bad.

Derek turned around to see me hopping around, holding my ankle, and spewing only the manliest of phrases like, "I want my mommy," and "My pinkie toe. My sweet, baby pinky toe is lost forever. I'll never be loved again…" You know, cool stuff that trends on Twitter and Instagram.

ABOUT THE AUTHOR

C.T. Walsh is the author of the Middle School Mayhem Series, set to be a total twelve hilarious adventures of Austin Davenport and his friends.

Besides writing fun, snarky humor and the occasionally-frequent fart joke, C.T. loves spending time with his family, coaching his kids' various sports, and successfully turning seemingly unsandwichable things into spectacular sand-wiches, while also claiming that he never eats carbs. He assures you, it's not easy to do. C.T. knows what you're think-ing: this guy sounds complex, a little bit mysterious, and maybe even dashingly handsome, if you haven't been to the optometrist in a while. And you might be right.

C.T. finds it weird to write about himself in the third person, so he is going to stop doing that now.

You can learn more about C.T. (oops) at ctwalsh.fun

 facebook.com/ctwalshauthor

goodreads.com/ctwalsh

instagram.com/ctwalshauthor

ALSO BY C.T. WALSH

Down with the Dance: Book One

The Science (Un)Fair: Book Three

Battle of the Bands: Book Four

Made in the USA
Monee, IL
11 January 2020